Immortal Again

-Supernatural Please Apply-

By

Matthew Smallwood

This book is dedicated to everyone who helped along the way. To the Morgantown writer's group and George Lies for pushing me. To all the special people in my life, they know who they are. Also, to you reading this and to anyone who ever took a chance opening a book they weren't sure about.

A special thanks to my editor Jeannine Thibodeau, God bless her and the work she did.

Chapter 1

Not so! Alas! Not so. It is only the beginning!
—Bram Stoker, *Dracula*

It is true, we shall be monsters, cut off from all the world; but on that account we shall be more attached to one another.
—Mary Shelley, *Frankenstein*

"Who are you then?"
"I am part of that power which eternally wills evil and eternally works good."
—Johann Wolfgang von Goethe, *Faust*

In some places—some rural places—the dark comes on differently. Far from city lights, night arrives like a black cloth placed over the head of a condemned man. Wadim Stoica, something of an expert when it came to the dark, believed West Virginia, his home of recent years, was one of those special places. Much like his birthland, Romania, the forest and mountains here whispered a secret to anyone alone or awake in the night.

The secret, revealed through raised goose flesh and a quickened pulse, happened to be the same one carried by cemeteries, certain old houses, and anywhere of great loss. The secret, which those who are living fear, says we are not the only ones here, not the only voyeurs. That maybe hidden things sometimes wait and sometimes listen to what we do. It is this sense of being observed that raises the short hairs and turns us toward an odd shape or a strange sound glimpsed in the shadows. It is the unmistakable sense of the other—of the unseen existing just out of our perception.

Going about his business, Wadim felt this other presence. He imagined he could almost turn quickly enough to catch one of the mythical creatures he sought. He took this as a good sign, a blessing.

The deserted fitness trail where Wadim started the ritual ran parallel to the main road. The trail, like a noose, looped around at the first fenced-off hill before turning back along the unpopulated forest. Like an empty stage awaiting performers, the countryside around the park resembled a single dark mass marred by distant porch lights.

Wadim, frustrated at the lack of results, skulked along the forested ridge, all but invisible amongst the tall trees in a charcoal jumpsuit and trailing cape. The elderly Wadim resembled a lost magician on his way to a child's birthday party. The face paint, caked on in poorly applied layers, turned his already pale skin even whiter, creating the illusion of a walking corpse. The expensive costume fangs covering his incisors stood out as he opened his mouth to breathe.

With enough supplies for a last attempt at the summoning spell, he found a litter-free spot on the forest floor. Wadim opened the fanny pack around his waist and removed a small plastic bag, holding the required chunks of raw beef. He tossed the pieces of meat into the woods and licked his fingers clean of blood. This gave his altered taste buds a hint of the final fear-soaked seconds of the bovine's life.

With the bag empty, he left it hanging from a low branch, allowing the leftover juices to drip onto the forest floor. The Internet site in which he'd found his information said the chunks had to be touching the bare earth. Wadim surveyed the area and deemed the job complete.

The Bloodening ritual, as the website called it, involved the summoning of the metaphysical and binding it to servitude. A commenter on the site claimed the spell came directly from King Solomon's own lost book of magic. The Bloodening required earth and blood to meet while the spell's caster dawned the apparel of the "damned." A stupid notion, and the more Wadim brooded on it, the more foolish he felt.

"A curse upon all your mothers for birthing you," Wadim growled at those who had posted the nonsense.

He had followed the instructions and offered the woods blood, and in return had received nothing. Disappointed in the lack of results, Wadim remembered when he had held the secret of immortality in his veins. Such a great span of days now filled the space between those wonderful nights and the bleak present. He often feared it had been nothing but a complex delusion— what the kids called "going momentarily off the deep end."

That wondrous time had been no bout of insanity, this he knew. He remembered the mysterious, nocturnal, traveling Romanian people of his youth, the ones who had given him the blood from their veins, which had transformed Wadim into a creature of the night. A creature blessed with eternal life, and a gift snatched away from him when an angry mob had burned his maker at the stake, an act rendering Wadim human once more.

Frustrated, he allowed the fresh night air to roll across the costume fangs before filling his overworked lungs. The unending warmth of the usually hot autumn shouldered oppressive weight upon everything. Even the dandelions drooped like defeated soldiers. The berry vines straddling the path resembled hollow brown husks as they surrendered every ounce of moisture to the heat.

Wadim paused to remove the false teeth. Despite a slight bowing of the spine, he still stood over 6' tall with a thin, delicate frame. His brown eyes had held onto some of their youthful glow, resembling fire-stoked stones. His hair had gone white decades before, and he hid this beneath a bargain-bin black dye.

When his chest ceased its heavy pounding, Wadim carefully descended the hill, sliding to the closest tree. Wadim repeated the process of controlled descent until he reached the parking lot. On the way to the last tree, his plastic cape snagged on an exposed tree root and ripped like cheap streamer paper. The shredded strands caught under his foot and almost sent him into a briar bush.

"You pig son, may your mother never know pride," he growled, his accent adding a course seasoning to the insult. The disappointment at yet another failure to contact any supernatural beings rattled him.

He stuffed the ruined cape in a trash bin near the path and gave it a good kick. Wadim took a handkerchief to the remaining face paint, hoping he didn't look as clownish as he felt. The cheap Halloween foundation came away easily enough, except for the wrinkles around his neck, where it hid in the creases.

A tingling shudder overtook him. This pulsing current struck like an electrical shock aimed at the sensory part of his brain. Instantly Wadim felt overloaded on pleasurable sensations. Like being lost to a powerful drug, his movements seemed exaggerated and slowed. It was as if he was experiencing a prolonged orgasm with no end. The muscle trembling, so intense, almost bordered on the painful.

Wadim's tongue rolled around in his mouth, threatening to restrict his breathing. He took a step and the woods spun around him as his equilibrium faltered. A large sycamore stopped him from falling over backward. The bark raked his back, but this small discomfort vanished in the torrent of everything else.

"The ether," he said, hardly able to form the words.

The ether was the ethereal cord connecting this world to the one beyond: the sudden drop of temperature in a haunted house and the inexplicable malfunction of certain electronics around cryptids was due to the ether and the supernatural things drawing on its power to manifest and affect the world of the living.

"Something must be there; I can sense you. Please show yourself. I beseech you, turn me if you can, let me join you."

Wadim wanted to say more, but the muscle movements escaped him. He had experienced the energy of the ether before, but never as strong as this, never so raw and direct. This interloping energy, the ether, had stirred the seldom-used extra sense he and the rest of his friends, the Fogies, carried for the supernatural. They were human now, yes, but they were also the autumn people—the folks especially attuned to the song of the unseen, because it was a tune once sung by every member of the group. Every supernatural creature of the night had a connection to the ether, and certain people and certain animals could sense this atmospheric shift, the same way some people could sense weather changes by the throbbing of old wounds.

In response to the current of dark energy, what sounded like every dog in the town began howling. Herds of fleeing deer thrashed through the brush. A chorus of owls and crows shrieked from the treetops as squirrels raced across the ground. The entire forest came alive in the wake of the energy.

Wadim parted his lips and moaned like a lover lost in a first kiss. With trembling fingers, he pulled his shirt down, to expose a mole-dotted throat bearing two small, circular scars, the marks in which the night first embraced him and made him one of its own years and years ago.

Alongside the rest of the Fogies, he had encountered similar spurts of the dark energy, but never anything like this. This was no haunted house or minor specter giving people the willies. No. Somewhere within a few miles, he could sense the genuine article, and the greatest of coincidences put him in proximity to sense it. Ridiculous when he considered all the weekends camped out at every Podunk graveyard in the state for something to finally happen in his own backyard.

"You're here. You're really here, but where?" he pleaded, almost in tears.

The tingling ended with an unexpected abruptness, no residual jolt, no ebbing trace, just gone. In its place came a bleak emptiness. In the aftermath his body replaced adrenaline and endorphins with aches and pains. While the sensation ceased immediately for him, the wildlife of the park continued to display a restlessness, and Wadim thought he understood the sentiment.

After a time, he decided this experience must have been a preview of what was to come—a foreshadowing of a possible change in his and the other Fogies' fortunes. He believed the rest of the group would be able to help him decipher the truth.

"Bronagh needs to hear about this," he whispered.

Chapter 2

The Old Fogies, as they liked to call themselves when out in public and online, frequented certain far-flung establishments. This was borne from necessity and rarely did this mean central air or breezy lakeside views. Because it happened to be within driving distance to all their homes, the Fogies picked Cathy's Truck Stop Diner as their unofficial meeting spot. The diner was open twenty-four hours, which suited their schedule, and the regular patrons were mostly truckers and tourists passing through—the perfect sort of people not to bother asking questions if they happened to overhear something strange.

The Old Fogies, thanks to the Internet, had become support group for former supernatural beings. In the banal world of mortals, the Fogies tried to help one another as they came to terms with being human, a transition that had become particularly difficult as they crept toward old age.

Bronagh O'Neil, the founder of the Old Fogies, greeted the dawn that morning by wrapping a shawl around her bony shoulders. She needed a moment to gather her thoughts before going to the diner to face the others.

She meandered a moment in the shade and tried to call her son once more. With his own job and family to look after, Michael Jr. rarely had times these days for his mother. She didn't begrudge him this. It's what life did to the sweet ones you loved. It gave them other things to care about and concerns beyond their parents. This was being an adult. Bronagh left him another voicemail, saying to call back when he could. She had something important to tell him but didn't want to do it over the phone.

With this little task finished, Bronagh made her way into the poorly lit diner and waited for her eyes to adjust to the gloom. For her, being inside the truck stop and restaurant was akin to being inside the unwashed dish towel of a soup kitchen. The remnants of past meals permeated the entire building. The greasy sharp smells of Folgers and a lard-laden griddle mingled together like two awkward strangers kissing on a dare.

The tired-looking server working the early shift stifled a yawn from behind the counter and asked, "You want some coffee, hun?"

"Ducof," Bronagh said to a confused glance. She blushed and tried a second time with a more deliberate pronunciation. "Make it a decaf, please."

She had been in the United States for many years, but the Gaelic dialect of her home still occasionally crept in to muddle her English, the language she would always think of as angry barking.

Her friends and fellow Fogies, Pyles and Conole, were sitting in a battered booth on opposite sides of one another. They sipped from steaming cups of the blackest coffee and looked bored.

Pyles the taller of the two, threw up a wave as he noticed her and offered a growling welcome. "'Bout time you made it, old girl. Christ, we were beginning to wonder if you forgot. You have to stop and take care of a feminine problem? Ha-ha-ha."

Ronald Pyles, the uncouth giant, had often been described as a Kodiak both in appearance and in a lack of any etiquette. Despite being on the other side of 60, he still came off as a corn-fed country boy. He carried a solid 300 pounds of muscle on top of a 6'6" frame.

Born in the hills along the Appalachian Mountains, Pyles thought it practically religious doctrine to wear camouflage year-round. He hid his face behind a bushy beard and stringy, unkempt hair. The centerpiece though and subject of numerous arguments was the large hunting knife Pyles kept strapped to his leg. The knife, or "bill opener" as he called it, created more headaches for their group than Medicare.

In his youth, Pyles had inherited the powers of a skin-walker. This gave him the ability to shift between the forms of wolf and man. He lived as both a beast and a human until a paranoid hunter had nicked him with a silver bullet, ending his time as a monster. As a parting gift, his nose carried the same qualities of a bloodhound. On a good day, he could take a single whiff and know if someone had used creamer in their coffee the morning prior. It could be an impressive trick when he wanted.

At her arrival, Conole scooted over to make room on his side. Conole, a fellow countryman to the Scottish-born Bronagh, was an elderly little person with an origin tied to the wee folk. Conole had been a sprite-like creature not so different from a leprechaun, minus the gold, of course. Then a solstice celebration by a bunch of druids had disastrous consequences to the land and its inherent magic. Conole became mortal and human happened to be the biggest casualty.

Conole came to their meeting wearing sweatpants, lace-free sneakers, and a red Windbreaker. He kept his white hair cut short, and his face smooth. His legs were bad and sometimes locked up, forcing him to use a black oak walking stick to get around. He avoided wearing shorts because they revealed the swollen misshapen look to his knees.

Conole checked his pocket watch, confirming the time. "Leave it to Wadim to show up late to the meeting he insisted on. Have either of you heard from the little prince since last week?" 'Little prince' was something Conole called Wadim when especially perturbed.

"Lord Fauntleroy has barely spoken to me; it's been blissful," Pyles said.

Bronagh swept away some stray food crumbs left on the counter. She took a napkin to a lingering stain of coffee and replied, "I talked to him Friday. At least I believe it was Friday." She ticked off the days in her head and once satisfied about the math, she continued, "Yes, it was Friday, he made a big to-do about planning something if the weather held."

"What do you want to bet he's dyeing his hair?" Conole said.

The waitress interrupted to bring everyone refills of a black oily coffee. Pyles watched her leave and dropped his head. He whispered through a jagged fence of beard hair. "Could you two maybe act like you got some sense? Try to ease up a bit when the normies are around. The less they hear, the better. I'm in no shape to outrun a mob."

Conolc added another packet of sweetener to his already sugary brew. "Pish-posh, Mr. Paranoid, you're fretting over nothing. No one is ignored more than the elderly. You should relax and enjoy being treated like the furniture."

This struck Bronagh as incredibly true, and she touched her mug against his. "Exactly, and when we leave, pay attention to how much I tip."

Pyles slurped at his coffee, careful not to burn his lip. "Did you hear about Carl Alderman?"

Carl Alderman had been a favored radio host on the local golden oldies station. He also covered the early morning swap shop on the a.m. channel. His signature enthusiasm for community events and witticisms made him a favorite of the retiree community. Carl had announced a bout of ill health recently and had taken some time away from the radio. He had been a fixture of the surrounding area for decades, and a lot of folks were praying for him.

Conole nervously shifted in the booth. "Did something happen to him? I had hoped he would make a recovery."

"The bad joke portion of his show never failed to make me smile," Bronagh said.

"He passed," Pyles replied, softening his voice. "Throat cancer robbed him of his speech, and not satisfied by this, it took his life."

Conole shook his head. "Another cruel death. It's the end to an era. I imagine they'll try to replace Alderman, but it won't be the same."

Pyles pointed at Conole to show they shared similar thoughts. "He was only three years older than I am, three measly years. It really makes me worry about how much time I have left if I don't do something."

Conole and Bronagh understood what he meant with this last statement. Wadim would have too if he had been there. Doing something about their approaching deaths had become the group's primary goal as they neared the golden years of decline. The age hill that once was on the other side of the statistics for disease and death sharply rose. Alderman was just one more example of how brutal the end could be. Their group knew there were alternatives but finding the means had proved near impossible.

Several city workers came in and shuffled over to a table by the door. Their arrival signaled the coming of the day better than any crowing rooster. The waitress returned and asked if they were ready to order, and the Fogies took turns with the single laminated menu. Pyles picked oatmeal and a side order of crispy bacon. Conole and Bronagh decided to share a plate of wheat toast and dry cereal. The waitress had just departed when Wadim, the final member of their group, entered the diner in a hobbling rush of excitement.

Done up like an over-the-hill sports guru, the tall Romanian blew in wearing a pinstriped tracksuit, set off by a pair of silver sneakers. His horrendously black dyed hair resembled a swimming cap made of tar. Tiny droplets of black sweat had trickled off the sides and stained his shoulders.

He dropped into the booth next to Pyles and shooed the waitress and her menu away.

"That's not very nice," Conole began, but Wadim cut him off by clearing his throat.

"Bah, we have things to discuss. Things of the most important variety—ether things," Wadim said. He placed a copy of the Eller County newspaper on the table.

Still reeling from the bad news, Conole ignored the paper and said, "Did you hear about Carl Alderman, the radio guy? Another good soul lost too soon."

Wadim spilled a fistful of salt into his palm and tossed it over his shoulder, creating a small mess in the next booth. "Sad. May he rest in peace. Let us pray his bad luck doesn't find us. I require you all to direct your attention elsewhere, lest we join him. We have matters of the macabre and amazing to discuss, most amazing."

The waitress noticed Wadim's actions with the salt shaker and frowned at their group. Wadim offered her a shrug of indifference and pretended as though it had been an accident.

Pyles glanced about to see if anyone had taken interest in the hubbub coming from their booth. "I just told these two about acting like they have some sense. I know you believe everyone ignores us, but you never know who's listening. How about maybe dialing back the creepy a bit, especially with the waitress?"

"A pox on your dialing back," Wadim said with a sneer. "I felt it, the ether, and it must have been a strong source. I went out to try to do that calling ritual. The one from the Internet, damn computers. It failed, but I tell you I felt something, something real, despite this. Something of the supernatural was there in Deer Rose. It was there, and it was using the energy of the other side, using the ether."

Conole nearly knocked his coffee cup over, trying to be the first to speak. "You're talking about the real thing, aren't you? I can tell by your expression. This isn't like walking by an old house and feeling a small shiver, is it? Could be it was the Moth Man or maybe the Flatwoods Monster? I've been to festivals celebrating both."

Pyles snickered as if either intentionally or unintentionally Conole had cracked a joke. "They have a statue to the old, red-eyed moth man in Point Pleasant. The thing has a killer butt on it. I'm A-one serious like a serious set of cheeks."

Bronagh tapped her chin. "Michael and I visited there once. We took pictures with the statue and kissed under the wings as if they were mistletoe."

"No," Wadim frowned, the act deepening the lines of his face. "This was no haunted house or giant moth. It happened in the middle of the city park, and every dog in town howled as if chasing the same giant squirrel. The thing must have been miles away, and I felt the pull. The kicker is I don't think it had anything to do with the ritual. I truly believe had the energy been any stronger, I might have passed out."

Pyles ran a finger through his beard like a comb. He mulled the statements over with a lip-pursed shrewdness. "Did you see any signs of what it may have been? This is all a little too coincidental for my taste. I smell something off about the whole thing. I mean we find something here. Not in a distant castle or a magic grove, but in small- town West Virginia?"

Wadim frowned. "Unfortunately, I didn't see anything, but I've been looking at the facts. This paper says that Saturday morning, a dead body was found inside a local shop. This death happened not even two miles from where I was standing that night. The paper doesn't say much, but the place is an antique store. Now use your imagination. We don't get many sudden deaths here, outside of automobile accidents and hunting mishaps. The paper doesn't say it directly, but it might as well say the word 'murder' in bold letters. This cannot be happenstance. The two are connected, I know it."

Pyles rolled his eyes. "I caught the end of a story on the radio. I'll grant you it's suspicious, but what's to say whatever supernatural creature accessed the ether hasn't already split?"

Conole raised his hand as if to be called on to speak. "If the ether was as powerful as Wadim says, maybe there's evidence. Though from our previous excursions to find the supernatural, I'm of the mindset the monsters like us are extinct. Like Pyles already said, why would it come here? I don't comprehend the reasoning. As far as the supernatural goes, I've always thought we were in a bit of a dead zone, no pun intended."

Wadim grabbed the paper off the table and wadded it into a ball. "Who cares if it came to rip the copper out of the wall? We need to figure out how to find this beast before it vanishes and to entice the thing to bring us across. Don't you see this is the ticket to ducking the reaper's scythe for good? Even if there's a chance, we must try, or we resign ourselves to cataracts and adult diapers. This is an endangered species of a dying myth come to us. I for one almost weep with joy, or would you rather join the departed Alderman?"

"Joy's great, bud, but what's your plan?" Pyles asked. "Do we just find a moth man or a wendigo or whatever, and ask nicely to change us? Assuming this is even possible?"

Wadim shook his head. He took a breath to calm himself before he started again. "We canvas the entire town until we find this beast. When we have it cornered, we strike a Faustian bargain for immortality, and just like that, say good-bye to heart pills and steroid creams. I vote not tomorrow, not this afternoon, but this very second, we depart. This may be as close a chance as we ever get. You must see this. Your vision is not so bad, is it?"

"But during business hours?" Pyles asked. "Wouldn't it be better to hold off until the sun sets? What creature can possibly be found in broad daylight?"

Conole broke his reverie to say, "He has a point about the sun setting."

Bronagh, already shaking her head to disagree, said, "Today is my apartment's monthly residents' meeting. There's no way I can reschedule without causing alarm."

Not satisfied at her response, Wadim retorted in a whine, "You can't be serious—a complex meeting? We've searched for a way back into the embrace of undeath, and here it is.

Handed to us as if on a silver platter, and you balk at it over an apartment meeting? We've all seen what the rest of the years may hold for our addled brains and worn bodies. How I have heard you Conole, you Pyles, and you Bronagh speak about escaping these mortal shells before it's too late. So now I ask: Were you serious in intent or was this just prater to fill the air?"

Bronagh stirred her coffee but thought better of another drink. "You dramatize too much."

Pyles scoffed, "Relax. We're all just as committed as you. We have prior commitments, things we can't blow off. I've already agreed to look after my buddy's gun shop for a couple of days. I get a big commission for any of the surplus ammo I can hock. For someone on a fixed income, this is kind of a big deal."

Wadim, wanting to make a point, smacked the table hard enough to rattle the salt-and-pepper shakers and bottles of hot sauce. "What's wrong with you people, do you not believe me? You must take me for a liar. Or have you resolved yourselves to your fate? Perhaps I've been wasting my time in this group. I could have kept this to myself." He spoke to them all, and yet stared at Bronagh.

Conole sighed and reorganized the scattered table items. "We believe you, but what if this beast is beyond reason? What if it's nothing but a passing encounter and already gone? It's better we treat it as nothing until we find out otherwise."

The waitress returned momentarily, pausing the discussion. She laid the separate checks under each of their plates and ignored Wadim's frown. The Fogies settled their bills and went out to the parking lot.

In the open air, Conole spoke first, leaning on his cane for support. "Wadim is spot on when he says it's an opportunity we should explore. It's silly for us to bicker and speculate until we know more. I mean, you can't be sure it's dog crap on your boot until you peek at the heel. I say a smaller group go nose around this antique store and see if there's anything in the aftermath, we can maybe sense."

"Dog crap on a boot—a lovely analogy," Bronagh said, hiding a small smile. Sometimes she it felt as though she wasn't the only woman in the group, but perhaps the last one on the planet.

"I like it," Pyles replied, telling them something they could have guessed. "Creates a certain universally relatable image. I also agree a smaller group might be better for drawing less attention. No point to go in guns blazing."

A minivan with an out-of-state license plate pulled into the dinner parking lot. A gaggle of kids climbed out the back door and followed their parents into the restaurant. The Fogies held their tongues while the kids took their time going inside. One little girl stopped to stare at Conole, as if beholding a real curiosity. Her frazzled-looking mother took her by the arm and gently led the child away.

The child called afterward, "But Mommy, I want to look at the tiny man."

With the coast clear, Wadim stooped down to address Conole. "Sounds like you're in, then. We'll do some snooping around and hopefully; the beast will come to us. Pyles, Bronagh, you be ready on the chance we need assistance. If we call, I don't want to hear any excuses about gun shops and committees. If this thing goes well, I'll only call once. After that, you'll be on your own."

Pyles belched and covered his mouth with meaty fist. "Duly noted. Is this meeting adjourned then?"

"Bah, I'm done here. Conole, you're riding with me, get your stuff," Wadim said. Because of the problems in his legs, Conole couldn't operate most vehicles. The Fogies were happy to drive him where he needed to go. He usually bounced around between their vehicles. Today was no exception.

Conole nodded. "I was charging my phone in Pyle's truck. I'll have to grab it."

Pyles flinched at a moving spot on the black top. The weevils were bad this summer, and they added small black punctuations to everything. Though harmless to everything but flour, they could still drive a person crazy when found in an unexpected place.

"Conole knows the gun shop's number, and I'll have my cell, so keep me up to date on how it goes. If we need to intimidate this thing, I can dig up a fifty-caliber revolver more than capable of doing the job." Pyles flicked a weevil off his forearm and then took two steps over so he could crush the small bug under his boot.

Bronagh flipped her hair to inspect it for bugs. She saw none there and shuddered at the idea. "I'm going to check the Fogies page and keep an eye on the community chat rooms. If I hear anything, I'll let you know. You guys be careful. I got this feeling. I don't know if it's premonition, but it may mean trouble."

They all had been touched in some way by their exposure to the spirit world, each in different ways. Their senses magnified in what they could detect. Besides occasionally sensing the world beyond, Conole could sometimes see auras and the taint of sorcery. Pyles could smell like a bloodhound, and Wadim's sense of taste was otherworldly, especially with blood. Bronagh could sometimes know when the specter of catastrophe was nearby.

Conole hitched his pants up and said, "Dear, you're going to spook us if you keep talking like that. I've already made up my mind though, so please…good thoughts only. To put you at ease, I'll call regardless of what we find."

He and Pyles walked to the truck to get his phone. Wadim lingered a moment as if more could be said. Bronagh's quiet shake of the head put an icy finality on whatever may have been building between them.

"Very well then," Wadim said.

He hobbled to his car and drove to pick up Conole. Pyles went next, squealing his truck tires out onto the highway. Once the others had departed, Bronagh pressed a heavy hand against her aching belly. The pain throbbed in her midsection as even the light breakfast digested. She hoped the unease would pass but her gaze lingered on the weevil Pyles smashed. She wondered if it signaled more dire things to come.

Chapter 3

The Stonewall Jackson Assisted Living Complex Bronagh called home sat at the end of a one-way street. It had been erected in the oldest section of Upshur County, which neighbored Wadim's Eller by about twenty country miles. The building resembled a scaling castle-like structure done up in the Crayola yellow sandstone of a beach resort. The complex had a photo-friendly parapet on the roof and an apple blossom tree by the entrance. Anyone going inside the building did so while walking alongside an impressive bouquet of lilacs, tulips, and bluebells. The more capable residents maintained the flower bed and considered it a point of pride. Bronagh liked to stroll past the flowers, sometimes stopping to smell their bouquet.

The interior resembled a poorly maintained boarding school for baby boomers. There were five stories with a pair of elevators moving between color-coded floors. The colors were designed to prevent the residents with dementia from getting lost. Ideally, as the floors went up, the residents' ages went down.

Until recently, the penthouse, as the residents jokingly called it, had been where Bronagh lived, but a week after her last birthday the complex's rules forced her to move. This, she feared, foreshadowed a terrible plummet, ending in childish curfews, dietitian-planned meals, and monotonous crocheting classes.

Most days the complex's activities reminded Bronagh of a bad soap opera. The figurative black-hat baddie in this case was relegated to one Bonnie Sweeten, a 60-year-old retired secretary, who sat on a small fortune from her late husband's life insurance policy.

Sweeten assumed this wealth guaranteed her certain entitlements. Entitlements she aimed to have, regardless of what it cost anyone else. She had even finagled her way onto the tenants' committee, the complex's form of a housing authority and the representation for the residents how life functioned there.

When Bronagh returned from her meeting with the Fogies, she spied a few of the other committee members in the lobby. Eric Brink and Lita Hardy were going over a stack of request forms with one of the nurses.

"Matching scrubs? Are they serious?" Eric asked. He shared a 'can you believe this crap?' expression with the young lady assigned to work the front desk. "And red, no less, because get this…it's a passion color, Passion? Really, only Bonnie no-good- Sweeten could come up with something like this."

Lita, always one for propriety, covered her mouth to laugh and replied, "Bonnie, Miss Royal High and Mighty. Mark my words…next will be formal dances and a 'who's hot and who's not' bulletin board. My granddaughter worries over the same thing, and she's in high school."

"Hot? I believe I would settle for lukewarm at this point," Bronagh said as she approached. "Tell me…have I missed something?" She worried for a moment Eric would crumple the request forms up like Wadim had done with the newspaper. Instead, he shuffled the stack around on the clipboard.

"Nothing but Bonnie and her latest round of insanity," Eric muttered.

Bronagh glanced at the nurse who looked perturbed as well. "What's this about scrubs? Don't tell me Bonnie has issues with the staff uniform?"

Eric turned the clipboard around for Bronagh's perusal. "She says a standard uniform would help the more addled residents from forgetting where they are. Don't worry—there's more. How about mandatory ID badges for residents, and a rule restricting the number of visitors allowed inside the apartments? I have a lot of grandkids; am I supposed to tell their parents they'll have to wait downstairs? That they'll have to take turns? This is paperwork for the sake of paperwork, and I can't see what her end game is other than to be a nuisance."

Bronagh had to read the forms again as the pain from her stomach kept blurring the letters. "We should ask these residents she's supposedly speaking for how they feel about this. We could round up a few of the others and see what they think about limiting the number of visitors."

Eric tapped the clipboard and said, "That's not a bad idea. We could try to get ahead of this thing. We can put our collective heads together and see if this is how the wind is blowing, but I have my suspicions."

"I'm thrilled to see you being proactive," Bronagh said. "Let's say everyone meet at your apartment in 30 minutes. On second thought, do you think we could make it an hour? I'd like a chance to freshen up a bit."

An excited Lita almost shouted, "I have some seven-layer cake in my room, left over from the community social. We can use it as bait to get people there."

Eric frowned. "My blood sugar was a little high this morning, so I'll pass on the sweets, but an hour is fine. I'd like to chat with a few more of the nurses about this uniform idea. If we can get them fired up, it will stack the deck more in our favor. Bonnie knows as well as we do that all expenditures on something frivolous is a loss somewhere important. She's doing this to spite us. Maybe if we shut this down hard enough, she'll calm down for a little while."

Lita and Bronagh left Eric talking to the new nurse coming on shift about red scrubs, and together the ladies shared a quiet elevator ride up to the fourth floor.

They parted ways with a light hug and Lita said, "I didn't want to mention it earlier, but you look pale. Are you feeling all right? Maybe a nap would be a good idea. I can come get you when everyone is ready."

Bronagh sagged and touched the purse pocket holding her phone. She wished it would vibrate with a message from Conole and Wadim. Her bad feeling from earlier had persisted like a case of indigestion. "I'm just tired is all. It's been a rather trying day already. Maybe I'll take your advice about that nap."

Lita grinned at this. "Okay, but Bronagh, we need you at your best. I don't know if it's the accent or what, but you're the only one who can keep us on course."

"I've always had a knack for staying on the proper path," Bronagh said, heading in the direction of her apartment. She paused at sudden cramp along her stomach. Bronagh pressed into the skin there and found a bloated, painful spot.

Bronagh pushed the idea of the disease away and fled into the preserved past of her home. Her sanctuary of an apartment existed as a cluttered museum to the happiest times of her 60 plus years of living as a mortal. Like a patchwork quilt, the gathered artifacts left over from a wonderful life gave off a certain cozy warmth. In the kitchen, she kept Michael Sr.'s collection of old coal lanterns on top of the cabinets, and the refrigerator held a collage of doodles and paintings from her grandchildren.

Bronagh had always found strength in the kitchen, maybe because food existed as a big part of the human experience. The act of cooking never failed to stir up memories of her first days as a mortal. Bronagh remembered the hazy, dreamlike state of being forced from the incorporeal specter without real consciousness into the corporeal body of a young woman.

For centuries, the O'Neil clan had been vexed because of the wrongdoings of an ancestor. Ever since, the spirit of the wailing woman haunted them whenever death and destruction were near. The clan suffered through plagues and misfortune for years, until a young soldier returning from war brought with him a sacred tome found in a distant land. The tome told of an exorcism, although it would prove an agonizing process of faith against fear. In the end, faith had been triumphant, but it delivered an unexpected outcome.

The young soldier, for all his preparation, hadn't been expecting a mortal woman to step forth out of the ghostly presence of the wailing spirit. The young Michael O'Neil stood before the girl and felt a yearning he would only speak of on their wedding night. He explored her angelic face with a mind no longer concerned with demons, ghosts, or family curses. He led her away from the church cemetery, and less than a month later, he brought the freshly christened Bronagh back in the white dress of a bride.

Bronagh made a cup of coffee and added a dash of whiskey from a flask. She checked her home phone for any messages, and seeing none, Bronagh went into the living room. Seated in the office chair, which she had salvaged from a yard sale, she turned the computer monitor on and waited for it to awake. In truth, computers would always confuse her. A class at the adult learning center had taught her enough to keep the Fogies in the digital age.

Bronagh set the mug of coffee next to the ceramic Halloween pumpkins she kept beside the mouse pad. She gave the computer another moment to work out the cobwebs before clicking on the icon for local news stories. It took less than a second before several articles about the antique store filled the screen. The story made the rounds through the different papers, and though the wording changed, the core details remained the same—a possible robbery gone wrong with a few items reported missing.

Bronagh minimized the story and did a search of the store itself. She found a couple of online reviews that called it overpriced and junk laden. One person accused the place of being a cover for the Black Cloves.

For curiosity's sake, she clicked on a link marked "Cloves," and found a popular brand of Turkish cigarettes and a blog about secret societies. The Cloves, or Black Cloves, as they supposedly liked to be called, sounded like the backwoods equivalent of the Illuminati. They were like the Shriners, but with more dark mysticism. Apparently, Jonas Kroitch, the owner of the store, had displayed a plaque behind the register showing a single cloverleaf with the center part missing, which the Internet swore was the Cloves' insignia.

Bronagh did some cutting-and-pasting and saved what she found under a hidden file titled RECIPES. She texted Conole the information on the off chance it would help.

Disappointed her phone didn't *ding* in return, Bronagh opened the main webpage of the Fogies. The home message greeted her with the usual picture of the Earth as it looked from space. The screen changed to show the same Earth encased by a large, elongated raindrop representing the ether. The image, as pacifying as it may have seemed, originated from a sketch by H. P. Lovecraft. Mr. Lovecraft, an author and known occultist, theorized the ether as an intangible embryotic-like cord connecting key points of the universe. While science disproved the theory decades before, nobody could have guessed how close Lovecraft came to the actual truth: The ether bound this world to the next and the beings existing between them.

The Lovecraft picture would stay up for 60 seconds before presenting a password prompt. Those who grasped the image's meaning and entered the correct response were granted access. The rest were redirected to a harmless gardening site.

The ones given access could speak in the forums and search through the archive of supernatural occurrences and sightings. In reality, the page came across as mundane because of how little it offered. Regardless, the site still provided the Fogies with a place in the online community. The website helped them to try to succeed in their quiet goal of once again escaping death by embracing the supernatural, a gift they had all possessed at one time—a gift even more valuable as the years continued to trickle away.

Of the quartet, Bronagh may have been the least sure about wanting to leave her mortal life behind, but she remembered how her husband had suffered at the end, the way his beautiful eyes held nothing but emptiness as he begged for help from the hospital bed. That had scared her more than anything. The terror on his face and how the cruel death had seemed a mercy before it was done.

Bronagh stretched her back and picked up the mug to find it nearly empty. "Slow down, old gal, or we'll be ass over elbows when the tenants come knocking,"
she said to dissuade the apprehension drying her throat.

She hated to admit it, but the alcohol had made her head spin. A nice little sit-down after all the computer clicking sounded like the perfect prescription for her anxious mind. Bronagh took the mug over to the couch and settled into the spot where the cushions always felt the softest. She put her phone on the armrest and waited.

She worried for the lads as though they were her own family. In a way, the boys had become exactly that. Bronagh knew the Fogies weren't the only such group of people out there, but theirs was proving to be the most enduring. Far too many of the others had ended up succumbing to the banality of a human life. Bronagh always believed their groups' longevity came from the geographical closeness they sometimes took for granted.

By coincidence, Wadim had moved to a nearby county from across the ocean. Having no families of their own, Conole and Pyles saw the trend of death in the chat rooms and wanted support beyond what the page provided. The pair had announced they were coming to West Virginia and found trailers within driving distance of Bronagh and Wadim. The rest became history.

The Moonlight Sonata ringtone ended her brief reminiscing fugue. Bronagh saw Conole's name flashing across her phone's screen. The stress had come in like the tide and receded in the same way. She hit the green answer button with her thumb. "Lads, you've nearly done me in, dragging this along."

Conole's whispered voice silenced her. The fear palpated his words like a panicked heartbeat. She had never heard him sound this way. "Bronagh, listen to me. Wadim's unconscious and may be dying. I'm not sure. There's someone here with us, someone dark."

Conole was terrified, and when he said "someone," his tone shifted to one of warning. There came a moment of dead air between them.

Suddenly someone screamed in the background and the call ended. Bronagh looked at her phone, not sure of what to do. She hit the redial button and listened as the just phone rang.

Chapter 4

Conole gathered his things from Pyle's truck and counted the weevils going across the pavement. He pretended not to watch as Wadim pined after Bronagh. It didn't look to be going well for either of them. Pyles stepped around to the driver's side door and his laughter boomed like the loud crash of a dropped dinner plate.

"He's like a dog with a bone. Why won't he give it up?" Pyles said with a chuckle. "Jesus, do you figure he's going start humping the air?"

Conole rested on the first truck step going into the passenger seat and grinned. "I doubt it, but what do you expect? That Bronagh is a genuine heart-stealer. I mean, look at what's she done to the two of you."

Pyles growled, his head turned slowly as if he had misheard his shorter friend. "What the hell do you mean by 'the two of you'? Don't lump me in the same boat as that moron."

Conole didn't see any reason to respond to such a half-hearted denial. They both knew it was fresh horse manure. The truth hid in every half-glance Pyles stole at her. Besides, a person in their golden years didn't throw chance into the wind and move to another cold-weather state for no good reason. Pyles had met Bronagh online, and then introduced Conole to the Fogies' site, and in no time at all, he suggested a change of scenery.

This great plan of romantic wooing, however, had never factored on there being another rooster in the henhouse. Wadim had also showed all the signs of a similar infatuation, which drove an unspoken wedge between him and Pyles. Bronagh must have seen the wedge, but maybe didn't know how to fix. Most of them were old enough to draw social security, and there they were, acting like lovesick teenagers.

"The charmer he is I think you'll live to fight another day," Conole said and together they watched as Wadim stormed off in an angry huff. "You lads could take lessons from one another."

Pyles grunted as he climbed into the rust bucket red truck and slammed the door hard enough to rattle the frame. "Laugh all you want short stack, but you have to ride with him now."

"I really hate when you're right," Conole said. He started off, and his friend's echoing laughter pursued him to Wadim's compact sports car.

Wadim leaned across the center console and unlocked the door. "Come on, I have a plan, but it will only work if we get there before they normally open," Wadim said.

Conole shimmied into the car and pulled the seat belt tight against his chest. "I can only move so fast. You know, you wouldn't die from showing a little consideration and patience."

Wadim twirled his fingers to show his enthusiasm at this. Through the rearview mirror, he watched Bronagh linger in the parking lot. Disappointment soured his expression. "Those people back there are fools—stupid, brainless fools. I give them opportunity, and they run screaming the other direction. Bah. They do not possess the sense the universe bestowed upon a mule."

Conole cranked on the adjusting lever until the car seat lay almost flat. This position helped his leg pain and let him marvel at the condition of the car's interior. The upholstery looked threadbare and somehow almost impressively, dust bunnies clung to the dome light.

Conole found a smile, despite the car's heavier mood. He grinned, considering how quickly his plans for the day had changed. No napping and reading for him. "Come on, that's not it. They don't want to get their hope up is all."

"Bronagh and Pyles doubt what I say, which in turn causes me to doubt them. They should have been clicking their heels together with hopeful glee. They are fools; I am not one for pursing a ghost." In most normal circles, this statement wouldn't have held the literal implication Wadim no doubt meant.

Even a dullard could see Wadim's scorned heart. He figured his good news would make Bronagh his. Sadly, this made Wadim the real fool. Conole felt for his friend but didn't see any way to mend the unrequited love.

Conole said, "Once we're able to identify what it was you sensed, they'll be more receptive, I'm sure. I mean, this is eternity we're talking about. This area has its fair share of legends and monsters. There are moth-men and giant-horned cats. I wonder if it was one of them you sensed."

Wadim pressed the button for cruise control and said, "Enough about giant moths. I would not put much stock in these things existing as we once did. I take them for legends and nothing more."

Conole, still staring out the window, said, "They may say the same thing about us. This is a ley-line state, who knows what has come calling? Pyles and Bronagh have been in the woods same as we have. They too have sensed the thinness there of the barrier between the living and dead, between this world and the next."

"I am done discussing those traitors. Now stop your prattling, I must organize what needs to be done in silence." Wadim cleared his throat and let the hilly drive have his full attention.

Amused by Wadim's potential scheming, Conole turned to stare at the grass covered mounds going by. There could be no luster in the heat, but along the shaded valleys, he could see an emerald kingdom of dark greens—some place momentarily protected from the scorching sun. This view reminded him of home, but the color wasn't lush enough, not near green enough. He let his eyes close when the road smoothed out. The jarring became tolerable, and before the first mile marker of the new interstate, Conole dozed.

Chapter 5

Sometime later, Wadim flicked the sleeping Conole's nose. "You can stop snoring. We're here."

Conole peeked through a single blurry eye to see traffic lights and billboards. With a yawn he asked, "Where are we?"

"Upper Main Street," Wadim replied. "Our business is there in that building on the corner."

"'Yesterday's Gone Antiques,'" Conole said, reading the sign displayed above the smaller crisscrossing black and red DO NOT CROSS police tape. "I didn't believe the constables used that stuff outside of the television. It seems a little tacky to me, like almost advertising for spectators."

Wadim's answer oozed contempt. "Remember, small towns such as this nurture inept public servants, politicians, and clergymen. This is our single advantage in this place. They foster inefficiency as if it is a resource to be hoarded."

Conole beheld the store and disliked it immediately. He couldn't say why, but the lettering and dusty window reminded him of a trap designed to lure people in. He figured this idea wasn't too far off from the truth, if the owner did indeed prey on tourists. Still, Conole believed it was a place he would have never visited otherwise.

Conole saw Wadim almost frothing with excitement and said, "So what's the plan here?"

They were parked in front of a walk-in bank, and as far as Conole could see, they were the only people around. Wadim's reply was a single finger tapping the digital clock face of his car radio. He dramatically crossed him arms, indicating a continuation of their wait, leaving Conole to wonder why he had been awakened.

The tepid waltz of the day continued in unabated silence. Wadim's plan must have involved an hour not yet arrived. The alternating rise of his thick eyebrows displayed the difficulties of Wadim's troubled mood. When probability finally saw fit to bring them into alignment as a straight line across his brow, he said, "That's that then, old boy. Come on and do your best to act as though we belong here."

"Should we poke around outside for a bit? Maybe look about and see if there's anything out here?" Conole asked.

Wadim scowled at the street and nearby businesses. "Only if we don't find anything within. I feel the taped-off shop is where all the answers lie."

The clacking of Conole's cane echoed along the empty street as he struggled to keep up. "But the door is going to be locked, and I doubt the police are going to come let us in."

Wadim scowled once more. "Do you believe I have not realized this? It's the weekend. Places like this seem to stay in bed outside the workweek. They won't rouse themselves until midday."

Conole looked up and down the street and thought the nearby shops looked more deserted than closed. Under blue skies, the place presented a picture taken directly from a Depression-era book jacket, almost to the point that Conole expected the café across the street to advertise war bonds. He wanted to ask about the relevance of waiting, but chalked it up to something better left unsaid.

Wadim sauntered up to the tape covered entrance and ripped the DO NOT CROSS barrier away. He glanced along the Deer Rose promenade to make sure no one had seen them. Satisfied no alarm had been raised, he shoved the shop's door. When it didn't budge, Wadim stretched his neck and said, "I had hoped the lock would be warn enough to slip open. I can circumvent the lock if I can find something thin to wedge in there—a sliver of either plastic or something metallic would be ideal. This is a skill I learned from the traveling people."

Conole continued to watch the street as a car came to a stop at the single traffic light. "You know, I had higher hopes for this grandiose scheme of yours. I'm beginning to regret agreeing to this."

A muttering Wadim bent over to examine the keyhole and snapped his fingers. "I need a library card…a credit card…anything of the ilk will suffice. Do you have a driver's license?"

"How much driving do you see me doing, ass? This trick you're betting the farm on only works on spring locks. This is most likely a catch bolt of some kind. All the police shows I watch have taught me this, along with the need of an alibi. I worry I'll regret not having one today."

"Bah, I forgot the expert is with me." Wadim snapped his fingers again.

Conole relented and searched through his wallet. He found a grocery store value card and placed it in Wadim's palm, like money going into a collection plate.

Wadim muttered what may have been thanks and slid the card into the doorjamb. He put his shoulder into the task and worked the card violently back and forth. His breathing intensified as the wood groaned. The cheap plastic card cracked and then broke as the door opened with a low snap. Mainly from brute force than skill they could now see the dusty, dark interior of the store.

"Success," Wadim exclaimed. "Here's your card back."

Conole took the pieces and put them in his pocket. "You're too kind. I wonder why you couldn't use a card of your own?"

Wadim's rushed entrance into the crime scene afforded Conole no time to consider anything else. He had to awkwardly hobble as he pursued the other man into what the police still considered a crime scene.

Inside the store, Conole perceived a hoarder-like clutter of everything ever abandoned on the side of the road. He marveled at rows of past their prime Amish cabinets, scuffed dressers, and battered coffee tables. Junk and knickknacks of every kind covered the shelves and floor.

The price of one such end table caused Conole to stop in his tracks. "Criminal just doesn't do these numbers justice. How did this guy get away with charging customers like this? How did he stay in business?"

Wadim flicked the tag for a $300 scratched armoire and sneered, "There is a sucker born every minute, which explains much of the computer age's problem."

"What is the search pattern for this landfill going to be? Anything real important the forensics gentlemen would have taken," Conole said, stooping under a rusty scythe.

Wadim grinned. "Forensics—you make me laugh. The nearest mobile unit is in Charleston over two hours away. This town would be lucky to afford them for the time it takes to cook porridge."

The *ding* of a message drew Conole's attention to his phone, where a text from Bronagh flashed along the screen. He pressed the "read" button and skimmed it several times. "Bronagh says the store may have connections to The Black Cloves. I guess they're like the Masons. I've read a smidgen about them, but Bronagh says to keep an eye out for signs."

"Will you stop playing with your phone and help me look? There must be something here that will tell us what happened."

Wadim took several boxes of paperbacks over by the window, since they didn't want to risk using the overhead lights. He flipped through a collection of *Frontier* magazines and a bunch of Western paperbacks while Conole tackled the romance novels.

They pecked over boxes like crows digging through a garden. Eventually, they settled on opposite sides of the aisles and tried to work toward one another. Conole and Wadim went along the top and bottom of every item, looking for the mysterious red herring. They worked through the inlay of a European bedroom set and the carvings of a zoo-themed toy box with no idea of what their prize would be.

A broken mirror suggested some sort of struggle, but this told them nothing they didn't already suspect. Conole coughed to clear a throat nearly filled with a cold spit.
"Come on, Wadim. We haven't found anything yet. We should probably go. I don't like the sensations in here. There's

something not quite aces about all of this," he said with a shoulder roll, as if to warm himself. "Did you notice the temperature change? I mean, there's no air conditioning ducts anywhere, and yet I'm covered in goosebumps. This place has been shut tight since at least yesterday, but it's like walking into a meat locker. It reminds me of that time we toured that closed hospital, what we felt in the morgue."

Wadim overturned a couple of antique washtubs to reveal dust bunnies and nothing else. "You refer to that waste of a Saturday, in which the tour guide blamed everything on devil worship?"

"That's it," Conole said, the realization striking him through the memory. "I believe a great deal of dark magic has been worked here. The real vile stuff you won't find through a couple of Google searches."

Thinking back to his own failed ritual, Wadim said, "And what do you mean by that?"

Conole shook his head and used his cane to nudge a shoebox full of campaign pins open. "Nothing—just that you have pseudo-rituals and then you have the real thing. I'm telling you this place has a stain to it like the real deal happened right where we're standing."

Wadim glanced about as if the evidence of such would suddenly materialize. He sneered at the bin of old lunch boxes. The top one showed a smiling puppy carrying a food bowl in its mouth. "Perhaps some of this junk carries the taint of demons, but we must find out all that we can about what caused the surge of ether. We must be sure. There can be no area left to chance, do you understand? I won't go back and tell the others we abandoned this because of misgivings."

Conole let the issue drop and squeezed in behind a line of old trunks set up beneath shelves of carved driftwood. Unable to shake the fear of witchcraft, he treated the contents of the store with trepidation. One of the steamer trunks lay flipped over on its side, the top smashed into half a dozen pieces. The brass fittings dented inward, as if struck repeatedly by a hammer. Amidst the wooden debris, he spied what looked like a murky boot print. Logic suggested whoever overturned the trunk must have stepped into the blood and left behind an impression of their footwear.

A black ichor, resembling dried maple syrup, looked to be mingled in with the blood. The ichor itself only seemed to have contaminated one spot.

Wadim hunched down and used his phone as a flashlight. He and Conole studied the scene for a moment before Wadim focused on the ichor. "What is that stuff? It smells like rotten garbage and waste."

Conole jammed a thumb under his nose to divert the worst of the odor. "I'm not sure. It looks like motor oil, but the way it's hardening…will you look at the size of that boot print? There's no tread beyond those two crisscrossing lines on the heel. What do you figure that means?"

"I am no boot expert, but the size is something of note," Wadim said.

Conole withdrew his phone and said, "Hold on. I'll snap a picture and send it to Pyles. I'm curious to get his take on this."

Conole sent several photos of the boot print it to Pyles. Once the messages had gone out, Conole turned his attention to the broken trunk where the craftsmanship suggested a remnant from a far different time. The inside contained a soft silky upholstery, almost like a nest, adding a lingering question about the previous contents. Someone had already ripped most of the fabric out, and a check of it revealed nothing, but some German lettering in the trunk's latches.

"Does this date mean anything to you?" Conole asked as Wadim continued to study the ichor. "Germany, September 12 of '45? I think the war ended in '45, but the 12 seems wrong. Except for this trunk and some overturned knickknacks, I don't see anything else destroyed."

An idea occurred to Conole, and he went behind the register to hunt for any kind of inventory list or sales record. He figured the police would have taken such things, and unfortunately, this assumption proved correct.

Again, Wadim gave no response and Conole looked over in time to see a strand of drool drip from his mouth onto the floor. Wadim had moved close enough to the ichor his nose nearly touched the stuff. To Conole's dismay, Wadim looked to be in the midst one of his of blood lusts.

Wadim's obsession with blood was a burden they had all come to accept as a side effect of his past. According to him, a person's whole life was in in their blood, and by tasting it, he could sometimes experience the key events. Wadim's fear of infection often helped keep his blood fetish in check. However, each passing year had dulled this phobia until it seemed he would drink from a hobo's arm if presented the chance. A few discussions within the group had motivated him to be more careful, but his dangerous urge still won far too often.

Sure, Pyles could sometimes smell things, the same way Conole and Bronagh could occasionally pick up a strange emotion or feeling. But none of those things brought about the manic-like shift in character as when Wadim tasted human blood. It reminded Conole of the poor insane bug-eating Renfield in *Dracula*.

Conole never imagined Wadim would want to taste the foul-smelling ichor. He hobbled over as best he could to pull Wadim away, but the size difference made this nearly impossible.

Conole dropped his cane in a rush to get between Wadim and the stain. "Are you out of your mind? Don't you dare taste that stuff! We don't have a clue what it is. It could be septic tank grime, and you're going to put it on your tongue?"

"Let me go," Wadim screeched. "That ichor is mostly blood, human blood. I'm almost sure of it."

"You sound crazy right now. Do not put it anywhere near your mouth. I'm warning you, Wadim. I'll tell the others."

If the threat meant anything to Wadim, he gave no sign. His mouth opened to show a tongue wet with anticipation of the blood. A fresh bead of sweat rolled down his face, regardless of the room's temperature.

Conole jammed himself under the taller man's shoulder and dug in. He tried to act like a carjack, keeping Wadim's lips away from the stain. "You're crazy. It could be arsenic for all we know, and you want to lap it up like a dog? What if it kills you? What then? No blood I know of smells like that."

"Allow me a drop. Then we'll have our answer, won't we?"

Conole couldn't hold the taller man at bay forever, and already Wadim's hands scraped through the print. Desperately Wadim tried to bring the liquid to his open mouth.

They might have ended up in a tussle right there, but the shop door suddenly slammed open, the sound of which broke through their impromptu wrestling match. Conole and Wadim noticed a middle-aged man standing in the doorway. The stranger held a key ring in one hand and his cell phone in the other. The man managed to look both astonished and angry at the same time.

The stranger wore brown slacks with a light gray jacket and eye-concealing sunglasses. His shaved head caught the light of the rising sun coming through the windowpane and reflected it like a halo of yellow fire. "Just what in the hell is going on here?" he asked, his finger working the buttons of his phone, while his attention never strayed from their embarrassed grimaces. "How did you get in? You look a little old to be meth heads, but I guess it takes all kinds."

"We're not meth heads," Conole said. "Come on. Do we look like drug users?" He offered a toothy smile to show his attention to oral hygiene and nudged Wadim to do the same. They let go of one another and came to their feet while they continued to offer friendly grins.

Wadim attempted to shake off the effects of the blood lust, but a strand of drool escaped the corner of his lip. Unabashed by this, he said, "You're not Jonas. Who are you? He told us to come by this morning so he could look at some Eleanor Rigby stamps."

The ease with which his friend lied stunned Conole. He watched Wadim fumble around in his pocket, making a show of drawing something forth. He searched for a moment and presented a small clear plastic checkbook with a single line of aged paper stamps inside.

"Jonas is dead," the stranger said, as if discussing something as casual as the weather forecast. "Someone murdered him, not far from where you're standing. Someone the police have yet to catch."

Conole and Wadim looked from the man to one another in a passable attempt at shock. Wadim turned as if to contain some wayward emotion. He battled the grief and said, "That explains why he wasn't here to meet us. I hoped he had merely forgotten. We found the door ajar and figured he was waiting for us in the back, but the police tape now makes sense. I'm sorry. Was he an acquaintance of yours?"

The bald stranger put the keys in his pocket and withdrew one of the walking sticks from the nearby bin. "I'm his silent partner, and I'd like to know how you two got in here. Especially since me and now the police are the only ones with the keys. I locked this door, so allow me to ask again…how did you get inside?"

When they weren't forthcoming with a reply, the stranger raised the walking stick like a bat. He continued to punch away numbers on his phone. "I thought the door looked jimmied open. Was this how you got inside?"

Wadim stepped around the broken trunk, and Conole shuffled backward.

Conole tried to straighten his attire to appear more respectable. Realizing Wadim indeed had something of plan with the stamp story, he said, "Sir, it's exactly like my friend explained. When we showed up, the door was unlocked. We figured the police tape was some stupid kids playing a prank."

The stranger divided his attention between them and his phone as he feverishly messaged someone. "I've been texting the police dispatcher, and they're sending a cruiser over. You two stay there, and keep your hands at your sides."

Conole frowned and rubbed at his thigh as it cramped. All the standing had started to take its toll. He had never heard of texting the police, but couldn't outright call it a bluff.

"Come on, we're senior citizens. Do we really look like cutpurses? I'm not exactly the best-suited fellow to load armoires into a getaway car. Why don't the three of us talk this over like adults? This is a simple misunderstanding. There's no reason to call the police and further muddy the waters."

Conole kept waiting for the sound of sirens to signal his impending incarceration. Wadim contributed nothing to the situation with his off-putting stare. A long shot idea occurred to Conole, and he decided it was worth it.

"We met Jonas through the Cloves. We're both members from the charter in Upshur County," Conole said. "Call them. They can vouch for us. I'm telling you we're not thieves—it's one big bout of bad luck for all of us."

Wadim piped up to say, "Especially poor Jonas, God rest his soul. He really wanted to see these stamps."

The stranger adjusted his grip on the walking stick. An uncertainty passed across his face. "I'm familiar with the Black Cloves. If you're a member like you claim, tell me the motto."

Conole didn't have a response to this, and the stranger's reaction said he expected as much. A short person in any social group inspired gossip, and the Cloves were probably no different. News of a dwarf member would have spread like a free phone app, and the stranger understood this right away.

Probably because if Jonas was indeed a member, then so was his partner.

"I figured you for bullshitters," the stranger said.

A police cruiser pulled up in front of the store without running the lights or the sirens. Two officers rushed from the car like the crime of the century had been perpetrated.

The stranger stepped aside to give them room during their charge. "I'm the one who called you," he began before the two officers were inside. "These men are here illegally. I would like them prosecuted for breaking and entering."

Wadim looked from to Conole to the goop still on his finger. He wiped a palm across his lips as his eyes narrowed. "They'll be fingerprints and hand restraints and there's a chance this stuff could wipe off."

Without waiting, Wadim jammed the ichor-covered fingers into his mouth. He pressed as far as he could without gagging and nursed at the gunk. The reaction came almost immediately, as Wadim fell over and convulsed. His eyes rolled back into his head and a white film sprayed out from between his sharp teeth. His legs spasmed hard enough to send a pile of hat boxes tumbling over.

Conole recoiled in horror. Though he had seen Wadim give in to the blood lust many times, he had never seen a reaction like this. It looked like the goop had caused a seizure.

One of the responding deputies radioed for an ambulance and circled the convulsing Wadim. His partner, meanwhile, kept the bald stranger by the entrance and took a statement.

Conole stood unnoticed amongst all the clutter, watching the nervous policeman try to stabilize his friend. He held his breath, waiting for whatever would come next. Conole inched his hand toward the pocket holding his cellphone. He hoped to send a SOS message to the others before his inevitable arrest.

He pressed the buttons to unlock the screen and scrolled through the short list of contacts. Conole clicked on Bronagh's number, and the option to call or message appeared. He swiped his thumb over the tiny envelope image, but the phone began dialing. The young officer who tended to Wadim caught the glow of the screen. He noticed Conole the same moment the light on the phone turned green as someone answered.

"Hey, you! Put that phone down and lower your hands," the deputy said, stepping past Wadim. "Hey, Armentrout, we got another suspect trying to slip away."

"The Cloves, trying to bring it back to life," a blood-mad Wadim muttered. His mind was no doubt elsewhere, in another place and time.

The stranger, still holding the walking stick, came on the heels of the other officer, the one called Armentrout. Something like sick delight sprouted across his ordinary features. Around the stranger and unseen by anyone else, small particles of light and dust shifted in the air. This gave Conole a momentary glimpse of the man's aura. It dripped with demonic taint.

Conole ignored the orders and moved against the wall. He brought the phone up and spoke. "Bronagh, listen to me. Wadim is unconscious and may be dying. I'm not sure. There's someone here with us, someone dark."

Wadim screamed and vomited a stream of blood and black film. The deputy's shoe absorbed a lot of the body fluid, and Wadim's thrashing became the focus of attention again.

Conole hung up and said, "He's never had a seizure before. I don't know what brought it on."

"It's a fetus," Wadim whimpered through teeth now smeared black with the goop.

With his last message delivered Wadim's trembling ceased, and he passed out in a pool of his own vomit.

The bald stranger toed through the ichor on the floor and gazed at Conole with a morbid pleasure. He played in the sick with his shoe, delighting in the mess it made. As the siren of an ambulance drew near, the stranger said, "Tell Lawson they said they were Cloves. They seem to know something about Jonas."

Conole's stomach churned as Wadim's body gave a final, violent jolt.

"Wadim, please say something or move if you can hear me," Conole said. With no reply, he could only wait as the police and the stranger came closer.

Chapter 6

Since Conole's call, Bronagh couldn't escape a terrible nagging guilt. She had been waiting for the other shoe to drop from the moment Wadim had shown them the newspaper. She should have tried harder to dissuade them from going in so haphazardly. Any situation involving a murder carried a dire air to it.

She attempted several more times to reach either Wadim or Conole by phone, but as Wadim's voicemail greeted her again, Bronagh suffered a long paralyzing second of indecision.

She paused in dialing Conole's number once more and instead pressed the button to ring Pyles.

His gruff voice answered after several seconds. He coughed and hacked in her ear. He growled to clear his throat and said, "Hello?" He somehow made the greeting sound both annoyed and accusatory.

"Sorry to bother you, but it's about the boys."

Worry had tied her tongue, but thankfully Pyles said the rest so she wouldn't have to. "Something went wrong, didn't it?"

In a rush, she explained what she could about Conole's cryptic statement. Bronagh knew she was babbling but couldn't help herself. Words poured out of her like rainwater coming out of a gutter.

Pyles, to his credit, accepted the news in a sullen silence. He hyphenated his listening with loud breathing that crackled over the receiver. "Conole sent me an odd text a couple of minutes ago. I don't know why, but I got this picture of a bloody boot print. I wasn't sure what to make of it. By coincidence, I've got the scanner on here and a breaking and entering came across the police bandwidth. I can't be sure, but it sounded like they said the Deer Rose City police were taking care of it."

Bronagh's stomach dropped at this, as if she stood teetering on the edge of a great chasm. "Do you think it was them?"

Pyles cleared his throat once more. "Old gal, I'd be really surprised if it wasn't."

She heard some chaos in the background as he juggled the phone around. His voice sounded distant for a moment. "Wait a second. I want to finish my computer search for the boot from the photo. It must have been important if they sent it to me."

"If you believe it's important," she replied, taking the weight of every idle second like a painful lash across her back. Bronagh kept hearing Conole's words repeat like a stuck record.

"Wadim's unconscious and may be dying, may be dying, may be dying."

Pyles's gruff rumblings returned, and he said, "Sorry about the wait. I also did a search for the city. I'm texting you the directions to the Deer Rose Courthouse. They have a holding tank in the basement. I figure if the police arrested them, that's where they'll be. I mean, these guys aren't exactly on the Ten Most Wanted List. Christ at the urinal, this is what Wadim gets for being in such a hurry. Would it have killed him to give it a day or two? Now he's caught trespassing in a crime scene. They may put him under the jail for this."

Bronagh cradled the phone between her ear and shoulder while she slipped her orthopedic sneakers on, the shoes she always thought of as her walking footwear. "What about Conole saying Wadim was dying? What do you make of a dark man there with them? You don't really believe Wadim could be gone?"

"No way, not our Wadim. He's a jerk; jerks live forever. Besides, I'd rather go by the police barracks before the morgue. In order of crap sandwiches, I prefer dry before soggy. The dark man could be anything. No point in speculating until we know more."

"What about this boot print they sent?" Bronagh needed a minute to make sure the tears weren't going to come. She wanted Pyles to distract her with something else other than morgues and police stations.

Pyles took in a deep breath. "Not sure if it matters, but it looks like a German- made infantry jackboot. Though the iron X heel ended with the Nazis. No one makes them anymore, because they're too hard on the feet. The things last forever, but they gave the soldiers hammertoe."

Bronagh quietly blew her nose. She blinked away the last possibility of tears and said, "They were going to visit an antique store, the perfect sort of place to find antiquated things like Nazi war boots. Weird though—a print would mean someone was wearing these."

Pyles snorted. "My thoughts exactly. The print is probably a replica, no one in their right mind would go about in the genuine article."

Bronagh knew it would be a bitter pill, but she said, "I can call all the nearby hospitals. They should be able to tell me if either Wadim or Conole have been admitted. I hope neither of them have matching prints on their backsides."

There was more static on the line as Pyles bustled about, doing who knew what in his cluttered trailer. "They wouldn't take them to the hospital unless they were hurt. I don't see this dark man killing them in broad daylight. You'll probably be wasting your time, but it's good to be thorough. While you're doing that, I can go straight to the store before the courthouse. I'll see if this dark man is lurking anywhere about. This means the gun shop will be on hiatus for a while."

Bronagh had a non-supernatural premonition of the mountain man going in angry and half-cocked. She could almost see him liking the idea of raising some hell, as he put it. Experience taught her he didn't like being told what to do. Sometimes this could have the opposite effect on his actions.

She did her best to keep her tone calm, trying not to be patronizing when she said, "Pyles, it won't do for anyone to go off playing hero. If you get there before me, you be smart and wait. Tell me you understand: No heroes."

The phone crackled again with static as the big man laughed. "Don't worry, love. No heroes here—fresh out. Tomorrow isn't looking good, either."

Not believing him, Bronagh said, "I'll call as many of the hospitals as I can, and you wait for me. I'm not kidding—there's something strange at work here. No gung-ho crap, be reasonable, and don't do anything that would put you in harm's way. The last thing we need is anyone else getting hurt."

A second of silence followed where she heard a mocking impersonation of her pleading. "No offense, old girl, but could be a gung-ho cowboy is exactly what we need. Those boys might have riled something up, something that needs settling back down."

Bronagh's free hand moved to her belly, where a knot of pain had gathered. "When the time comes for a shootout, I'll let you know. A cowboy you most certainly are not. So tell me you're going to play this smart," Bronagh said with the firmness of a frustrated parent at the end of their rope. She heard the harshness in her words, but couldn't help it. Worry and stress sometimes shortened her temper.

A long pause over the line made her think he had maybe hung up. She didn't need any special sense to detect the irritation when Pyles finally responded. "All right, we'll do things your way for now. I'm not a child though. I'm not Wadim. I can handle myself. You don't need to mother me."

Alone in her apartment Bronagh mouthed the word "ass." Knowing it to be probably futile, she offered a final piece of advice, "You do whatever you want, but you might want to remember to take that knife off your leg before walking into the police station."

Bronagh didn't wait for a reply. She closed her phone and ended the call.

She gathered her keys and purse and rushed from the apartment. She fast walked to the elevator and mashed the arrow for the lobby until her finger hurt. The elevator doors opened with a lengthy groan and a ding. Inside Lita stood with a commercial- sized coffee maker clutched in her bony arms.

Lita rocked the coffee maker to her chest and said, "Why, I was on my way to your room. Do you think this contraption is big enough? I borrowed it from the activities room."

Bronagh had hoped to slip past everyone and apologize later, but the fates had conspired against her. She fumbled for a suitable explanation and said, "I hate to tell you this, dear, but something has come up. I'm afraid it requires me to leave. There's not a lot I can say except I'm sorry. It involves a trip to Deer Rose."

Lita changed her grip on the industrial sized coffee maker. She opened her mouth to speak, but before a single sound materialized, the elevator doors closed between them.

"Oh bother," Lita said through the metal of the elevator. The doors dinged open, and she reappeared, looking flustered and embarrassed. The coffee maker's cord dangled between her legs like a tail as she struggled with her grip.

Bronagh placed a foot against the doors to keep them open. She helped take the weight of the coffee maker until Lita righted herself. Together, they tied the cord in a knot around the machine's middle and shared a grin at the absurdity of the moment.

Bronagh said, "It is sort of an emergency. Will you please give the others my apology?"

Lita set the coffee maker on an empty lawn chair some thoughtful soul had placed by the elevator. "Bronagh, that's terrible. Tell me it's nothing with the grandkids or your son?"

The look of genuine concern on Lita's face warmed Bronagh like hot cocoa on a cold morning, but she couldn't permit it to continue. "No, it's nothing like that—he and the grandkids are all fine."

Forgetting about the coffeemaker for a moment, Lita touched Bronagh on the arm. She leaned in and whispered, "Most of us aren't trying to pick up a cause with the few good years we have remaining. With you, though, it's like you're looking for a fight. We need you there to remind us why we're doing this. Why should we care?"

The elevator car arrived, and Bronagh went inside and pressed the button for the lobby. Lita lingered by the wall, showing an indecisive fear as she turned to consider the empty hall.

"It will be all right," Bronagh said. "Fretting won't help with anything. You don't give yourself enough credit, Lita. You can be feisty when you want to be."

Lita blushed at this. "I'll figure out something; you go take care of your emergency."

"Thank you, I will," Bronagh said as the elevator doors mercifully closed. She hated to be dishonest, but she had little choice. The slow ride in the lift left her alone with the guilt she had begun to accumulate like dust in a long-shuttered home.

The short walk from the front lobby to the parking lot taxed her reserve of strength. She stopped by the flower bed to catch her breath and her own allergies brought on a series of coughs, the last of which Bronagh caught in a trembling fist.

She stared in horror at the webbing of her fingers, now dotted with blood. Bronagh swooned on her feet and considered the blood and its unsettling implications. "A sinus infection, and that's all," she said, as a taste like the hard water from a hand pump crawled along the back of her throat. "Just hold it together a little longer, old gal," she said. "Just a little while longer, please."

Chapter 7

Pyles and his loud truck arrived in the town of Deer Rose like an unexpected bout of food poisoning. With a lot of racket, he parked the battered Chevy in a gravel lot at the back of the county court house. He settled into a space near the end of the last row and the truck's engine gave a final, warbling roar.

The angled spot afforded him a view of the three police cruisers lined by the entrance of the barracks. He could also keep an eye on the road and the looming arrival of Bronagh and the broom she would assuredly fly in on.

After finding nothing at the store but more police, the only other thing to do was wait and watch. Though there wasn't much to see. On the other side of his windshield, average Joes and plain Janes came and went.

Pyles's powerful nose didn't have the *oomph* it once did, but he could still get a fading aroma off some of the normies passing by—the tide of folks who swathed themselves in bargain-bin shampoo and flavored coffee. The cold hard facts were people literally stunk, but the majority at least tried camouflaging the odor with perfume and cologne.

If a sharp sniffer didn't define being cursed, Pyles reckoned nothing did. The people, the animals, and the buildings were saturated with excrement. They were sautéed in scat until it infused everything.

When the foot traffic going in the courthouse died off, he climbed out of the truck. Pyles sniffed around for the familiar stink of Wadim's hair dye. At the cost of a migraine and blurry vision, he could focus in and separate the multitude of scents. Once found, he could follow the scent like an old blue tick hound.

He had hoped Wadim's hair oil would draw him to the boys like flies to crap, but the parade of people muddied the air. To help with the process, he opened his mouth and allowed the thousands of different smells to roll over his tongue. The odors came like a sampling from a buffet of the overly sweet and the bitterly sour.

Along with the pomade, he also sniffed for any trace of Conole's Ivory soap. Because of course Conole used the soap with all the Irish folks in the commercial.

In the gutters of the courthouse, a mother bird fed her babies the regurgitated remains of an earthworm. The scent brought him the taste of the worm's sulfurous guts.

He walked across the graveled lot and tilted his head back like someone about to cross deep water. He found himself on his tippy-toes in effort to get above all the carbon monoxide rolling along the streets. Pyles pushed his nose until his eyes watered and blurred under the strain. His vision filled with black spots, but the faintest scent of Ivory soap and hair dye emerged from the melting pot of the town's fragrances.

His internal compass sent him toward the bottom of the courthouse, all but confirming his and Bronagh's suspicions. The combined scent of both men grew more pungent around the windowless basement. This was where Pyles imagined the holding tank would be.

Pyles despised waiting, especially since he was sure he had found Wadim and Conole. He especially hated killing time because spare seconds were a commodity none of the Fogies possessed. He didn't much care for the standing around and he blamed Bronagh for trying to unman him. Lord Almighty did that woman have a mouth on her.

Like his dad's dad, old Pap Clay would tell them when they were young, "A woman won't always say she loves you, whether she really does or not. But boys, there hasn't been one born yet who wouldn't crawl over five miles of broken glass to chide you good for doing something foolish. You better believe that."

Pap Clay, arguably the smartest man ever, had bestowed upon Pyles the best piece of advice ever. He had taken Pyles aside on his thirteenth birthday and said, "Your brain, your pecker, and your stomach all ride the same train. They all ride together, and every second of every day, one of them is trying to oust the others, so it can be the conductor. It's a hell of a scrap most times and believe me, between the three of them, they can usually keep the train on schedule. But if you ever get in a real pinch, and I mean the kind that can lead to a cold grave—you put your ear to your gut and take heed. The gut is the tracks that keep the whole damn line of cars from running off the rails. The guts don't lie, and they don't sugarcoat."

"Damn right," Pyles said at the memory.

The old and odd recollections had been coming from a strange, unexplored side of his mind. Pyles thought his aged brain had become a lopsided, shelf-lined with jars full of forgotten memories. Every so often, something caused the shelf to shift, and a jar would tumble down, spilling a lost memory across the floor of his consciousness.

Like the recollection of Pap Clay's last birthday cake coming on without any provocation. Pyles hadn't thought about the cake in almost 50 years, and yet he could remember the homemade pink icing. He licked his lips and wasn't surprised at all to taste the same tart strawberry flavor.

The clock on his phone said 12:15 p.m., and he couldn't believe time had already moved so much since Bronagh's call. If Wadim and Conole were inside, they would have to make their peace with at least one cold bologna jail sandwich before anything could be done. Pyles enjoyed this delicacy himself a few times when he was a resident of a drunk tank. It wouldn't kill them, but he didn't envy any toilet they would be passing for the next little while. It didn't make much sense to let more of the day slip away to useless waiting, but remembering his pap's advice, the guts told him to go slow.

Pyles begrudgingly strolled back to the parking lot to wait on Bronagh. His tumultuous mind struggled under several conflicting emotions. The unexpected memories coupled with an overworked nose didn't help. A certain question kept reoccurring to him, and thus far he couldn't answer it in any satisfying way. Minus all the bullshit of their recent back and forth, would Bronagh still be so concerned if he were in trouble instead of Wadim? Did their lives hold equal value in her eyes? He wanted the scale of rational truth to tilt toward *yes*, but the balance remained frustratingly somewhere in between.

While pondering the question and the two possible responses, his nose, which couldn't ever really shut off, wrinkled at an odor beyond wretched, an odor he had skimmed over in his search, but couldn't ignore as the sun drew its foulness out. He floundered for some context to justify the rotting stench of decaying flesh wafting in to fill both nostrils. He couldn't comprehend a reason for its being, unless something had suddenly dropped dead and rapidly began decomposing in a pool of its own sick.

The mystery stench lay like an alligator, waiting beneath the surface of thousands of other scents. Pyles obsessed over the off-putting stink. He pursued it to a blackish smear on the sidewalk leading to the barracks.

He spotted an imprint of a sneaker tread too small to come from anything but a kid's shoe. Conole wore a modified sneaker and the print looked to be about the same. It could have been with quick thinking that Conole had intentionally ground the goop into the cement, knowing Pyles might sniff it out. This idea might have been far- reaching, and yet it also digested easily enough into everything else.

Whatever the stain happened to be, it didn't look to be doing well in the sun. Its rim had already started to brown and flake like a scab. Soon it would be another nameless smear on the sidewalk. The smell brought forth apprehension, and Pyles took in his surroundings with a little more unease. This fragrance carried death and something else he could only classify as age or ancientness—the smell of an old slumbering grizzly in its den.

His family jewels retracted as if plunged into January's iciest pond and next to the cold, fear was the only other explanation.

In the eyes of a man who once shed his skin for a wolf's fur, he figured life had few surprises left. He couldn't have been more wrong, though, and Pyles accepted this a second later, when the impossible played out before him. He didn't want to call it a vision, because there didn't seem to be anything religious about it. But the mirage, if that's what it was, must have been coming from somewhere otherworldly or else he had lost his mind.

Between the courthouse and the neighboring probation office, what resembled an old black-and-white film scene played out above him. The scene materialized from thin air, like a window torn open between the land of the real and the land of the two-dimensional celluloid. At first Pyles believed his overworked mind had fractured under the stress. Like police dogs pushed too hard, he had smelled himself into a mental breakdown.

Pyles immediately recognized the setting of the film to be the all-too-familiar metal slab and high arcing Tesla Coils of an evil scientist's laboratory. He discovered a nauseating vertigo effect if he tried to stare through the illusionary screen to the real blue skies beyond. He rubbed his eyes and shook his head, but the phantom film remained.

His interest piqued at the notion of sidestepping around the disembodied screen to see what would happen. But even widening his stance brought on a seasick-like nausea. He also harbored the strange fear of somehow tripping and falling headfirst into that grainy, black-and-white motion picture universe. It screamed illogical and foolish, and yet his gut, which was temporarily calling all the shots, said to be careful— very careful. Something strange and possibly dangerous was happening here.

The mirage flickered and the unseen camera moved into the heart of Dr. Frankenstein's lab as depicted by countless horror films. Pyles hadn't gone deaf to the chirping birds perched on the courthouse roof or the far-off roar of an industrial-sized riding mower. No, the volume of the fluid city hadn't diminished, but the hissing, clicking of the film's reels mingled with these normal, everyday sounds.

A flash of sodium bulb lighting on whatever soundstage housed the phantom production cast a quick radiance across the lab. In the brief glow, Pyles spied a figure concealed under the white sheet of the table. Leather straps bound the sheet-covered body to the metal slab and in the long, gray shadows, cast between strokes of lightning, and the sheet stirred.

Every time the view inside the film shifted, Pyles swayed as his equilibrium tried to adjust. His stomach protested, and his sense of balance faltered.

"I must be off my rocker, or that stuff drugged me somehow. That must be it, I'm high off my ass and hallucinating all of this," Pyles said, hoping the statement would somehow set him at ease. The logic held, but he didn't feel as if he was high. He didn't feel anything but the odd sense of being watched.

The angle in the film changed once more, and the camera moved in for the inevitable close-up. The view crawled across the terribly designed set to further reveal a dark stirring on the table. An arm, grayish in hue and clad in military fatigues, slipped free of the restraints. Pyles held enough knowledge of the horror genre to know this was the part where the doctor and perhaps the hunchback Igor were supposed to face the creature they made. The pair would shriek with delight, "It's alive, it's alive, alive!"

This declaration would act as a cutaway and a change in locations, but Igor and the good doctor must have been axed for budgetary reasons. The scene remained focused on the body under the sheet. The shot lingered long enough to ruin any pretense of being entertainment.

"Save on casting and then blow your wad on creature effects, sound reasoning," Pyles said, unaware he had inched his way closer to the screen.

His threshold for accepting the unnatural reached well beyond the normal tolerance, and yet despite his experience, Pyles feared for his sanity. This scene from a low-budget Frankenstein horror film confused him, and no amount of blinking dispelled the illusion. Like a nightmare, he knew the monster, the boogeyman, would be forthcoming, and that's when the film would take its dark turn.

On the table, the stitched-together monster found the belt strap going across its broad chest and with an unholy strength tore it away. The reanimated corpse shook its powerful legs and the sheet draped across it tumbled onto the cement floor. As if sent by Zeus, the fake lightning flashed a second time, displaying just enough for Pyles to see the jackboots covering the monster's feet. The camera focused in on terribly inhuman eyes.

Before he could discern anything more, the movie screen disappeared. At the same terrifying moment, Pyles realized he had come within inches of touching the illusion. A strange hypnosis had almost drawn him into the movie and possibly a fate worse than death in the celluloid world.

The seed of a sprouting worry overtook him, and Pyles saw no way to stave off its growth. He knew seeing this movie meant something. He had never experienced a vision before, and wondered about its purpose. The feeling of being observed dwindled, and he wondered at the cause.

Not sure of what else to do, Pyles went back to the brown smear, which had almost completely evaporated in the blazing rays of the sun. A large fly looked to be going into its death throws in the middle of the last liquid drop of the stain. Seeing this caused a new worry to take root in his troubled mind.

"Lord, Conole, whatever this gunk is, I hope you were careful and didn't get any of it on you," Pyles said, watching the fly shudder a final agonizing time.

Chapter 8

Conole was a fellow of short stature, and he still found the cell to be extremely close quarters. It held the dimensions of a mall kiosk, and for reasons unknown the metal toilet came without a seat. The question of what he feared a prisoner could do with a toilet seat hounded him.

The arresting deputies were foolish, but at least had enough sense to call an ambulance for Wadim. Up until now, all the senior officers Conole had met at the courthouse floated between either apathetic indifference or open hostility. They growled when he asked after his friend's condition and ignored his request for a phone call.

He must have pressed the issue too much for one obese officer's liking. The fellow slammed his nightstick down across the desktop where Conole had to stand on a chair to be fingerprinted. The childish tantrum came within an eyelash of striking Conole, and nobody in the room objected.

They finished his fingerprints and snapped his photo before escorting him down a short hall to a pair of empty cells.

Before closing him in, the officer demanded his shoelaces and belt. Once Conole handed the items over, the officer tossed a partial roll of toilet paper onto a bunk mounted into the wall.

This escorting deputy turned out to be the same one who had initially overlooked Conole in the store. The young deputy acted decently enough, but the mistake of allowing a suspect to linger so close had clearly rattled him. He seemed distracted as if reliving the arrest but with a more fatal result for his mistake.

Conole felt responsible for the boy's sour mood but doubted the situation could be remedied. "I just wanted to say thanks. You probably saved my friend's life back in the store by not hesitating."

The muscles in the deputy's jaw tightened hard enough to pop as he gritted his teeth. "It'd be in your best interest to stay quiet and do what you're told."

"All right," Conole whispered. "I'll shut up."

Without another word, the officer secured the cell. Conole hitched the waist of his trousers up and shuffled over to the metal bed to wait. The accommodations included little besides a pair of bunks bolted directly into the wall, a dirty, crusty steel sink scabbed over with vomit, diarrhea, or a combination of the two. A ceiling- mounted camera in the hall kept an eye on the cells. It looked to be of the older variety, and Conole doubted the quality of the video feed. Conole started to wave but thought better of the idea.

The crumbling stone walls of the cell were dominated by the carvings and graffiti of bored prisoners. Inked claims of innocence and penned-in games of tic-tac-toe went from the floor to the ceiling.

Directly across from where he sat Conole spied an ominous bit of black lettering. This graffiti, unlike any other, had been drawn in a bold, clear script like the warning label for a dangerous product. The cell graffiti said, "Beware the snakes who serve goats, they bite and wear badges. Pray for your soul."

Beneath this the artist had drawn a snakelike creature coiled to strike. This snake had the face of a bulbously human male. The picture bothered Conole in the way it came from both a talented and profoundly disturbed mind. The longer he looked at it, the more unsettling the image became.

Cell time defined slow time and he could nothing but fret like a nervous hen about Wadim. Concern for his friend made sitting still impossible. Wadim had been awake when the paramedics had hustled him into the back of the ambulance. That much was certain. The more vocal of the paramedics had cringed away from the goop covering their patient. While one trooper rode in the ambulance with Wadim, the other officer had cuffed Conole and put him in the back of the squad car.

Locked in the hot car with no air, Conole sniffed something horrid. He happened to spy the black goop marking the sides of his sneakers. Out of instinct, he had come close to wiping it on the patrol car's floor mats but suspended the urge with the greatest of restraint. If he couldn't leave breadcrumbs like in the story, then maybe he could make do with smells. Pyles could be a bloodhound when motivated.

So on the way into the courthouse, he had paused as if in pain and did his best impression of someone cleaning dog crap off their shoes. Conole twisted his feet as much as he could with the officer's hand on his shoulder and raked the goop across the sidewalk. This transferred most of the ichor and a lot of the stink went with it. At least he'd succeeded in not tracking the foul stuff in with him.

Time in the cell meandered in long drawn-out seconds. A loud, braying laughter would penetrate the thick door and let him know life continued despite his internment. Doors banged, desk drawers slammed, and Conole could only worry about Wadim and the demonic energy in the store. The Fogies had seen much, but they had avoided the darker parts of the universe.

Conole heard the heavy lock of the hall door turning and imagined it would be the deputy. He didn't expect a disheveled Wadim to be led down to the cell.

Wadim looked and walked like the living dead as the officer guiding him hovered close. The pair moved in silence, and Wadim, in his dazed state, stopped at the first vacant cell he came to. The deputy grunted and said, "Keep moving. The chief wants you and your accomplice to cozy up with each other for a little while."

"Wadim, are you okay?" Conole asked from the other side of the bars. He looked at his friend's glassy stare and tried to rationalize what hospital would release him in such a state. "He shouldn't be up and walking around. I want to go on record as saying this is neglect of the highest caliber."

The deputy seemed more concerned with the errant ball of fuzz stuck to his lapel. "The tough guy over here got to the emergency room and decided he didn't want any treatment besides some iron pills."

Conole couldn't help but gag at the smell coming from Wadim. "And you, as a constable of the law, believed him to be in the proper mindset to make such a decision?"

The deputy placed a Folger's Adams key in the cell door and opened it just long enough for Wadim to take a short step inside. "He was lucid enough to tell us the year, his name, and a little about his medical history. It appeased the doctor, so I guess it's good enough for us. If he's not crazy or unconscious, he can refuse treatment so long as he signs a waiver."

Conole made room on the bunk so Wadim could sit. He didn't like the way his friend seemed to be in a fugue state. "And I suppose you made sure to get a copy for yourself?"

The officer smiled. "Two copies, both signed and witnessed. Besides you should be thanking me for the bunkmate. Protocol dictates separate holding tanks for possible codefendants, but the chief said you can keep an eye on him on the off chance he has another fit."

Conole wished he were big enough to reach through the bars and throttle the man. "So if I yell, then you'll come running to help?"

With long, drawn-out groan, Wadim surprised them by speaking. He leaned back until his head rested on the cold stone and closed his eyes. "That will suffice, Conole. No need to antagonize any further. It's like they say: I am fine as paint. Just got a bit dizzy is all. I imagine I let myself get too worked up."

The officer snorted, "There—from the mouth of babes. You yell, and we'll come running."

With the cell door secured the officer strolled away whistling a song from *The Wizard of Oz*. In the wake of being locked in, Wadim stared at the ceiling. "Before you say anything, do you think that camera watching us has sound? Can I talk freely?"

Conole shimmied to the corner of the thin blue mat serving as a bed and peered at the antiquated camera suspended outside their cell. He guessed it could see the bunks, but not much else because of the angle. He didn't see any sort of speakers or microphone for picking up sounds.

"I severely doubt it. I don't know much about the subject, but its appearance is as outdated as a tube television. I figure we're safe."

Wadim groaned and burped up something brackish onto his shirt. He said, "If you were to chop me up and feed me to wild canines, I would still not feel as bad as I do now. I lay a curse on the maker of those iron pills. They are not going down easy. My stomach is doing summersaults. Pray I am done throwing up."

"Yeah, it's the iron pills causing this and not that stuff you tasted."

Wadim shrugged. "Compulsion is a terrible thing. Judge not lest ye be judged."

Conole's leg throbbed from sitting on the bunk, but this was the least of what angered him. "You numbskull, why did you ever leave the hospital? You were throwing up blood, and who knows what else? There wasn't that much of that stuff, and still it's somehow caked all over you. It's like it reacted with your insides. I don't understand how you're even up and walking. You acted like an imbecile in the store."

Wadim glanced at the front of his shirt and brought the filthy fabric up to his trembling face. "Well, this lingering smell explains the repugnant way in which I was treated in thc ER, and I feared it was my Romanian accent."

Any humor from this joke faltered against the unhealthy glow of Wadim's already pale skin. The veins of his arms bulged from dehydration and a nasty shade of blue resided on his lips. Conole didn't care for the corpse-like appearance of his friend. He looked like the walking embodiment of death.

Wadim checked the rest of his clothes and saw similar smears of vomit. "My stomach is cramping. I need water and see nothing but this deplorable sink. I would be better off quenching my thirst from the toilet."

Conole held his questions until Wadim had a chance to drink several cupped handfuls of the dreaded sink water. Wadim ran wet fingers through his hair and tucked the wayward strands behind his ear. The self-grooming did little if anything to help his appearance, but he acted more alert because of it.

"You were babbling in the store. You said a lot of things, screamed them, in fact. You really did a number on my constitution. Was it worth it?" Conole asked.

"Forgive me for my indulgence. I regret the worry, but that goop showed me many things, some of which my mind is still reeling over. I don't want to discuss it here. Though I tell you—this is serious business we have found ourselves in. If what I saw was true, we are dealing with cultist."

"Okay," Conole said. "But I want to be there when you tell Bronagh the story and how you came by this information."

Wadim scowled but nodded to this succession. "If we live to tell her."

Before Conole inquire further about this ominous statement, the corridor door opening interrupted them, but on this occasion, it slammed against the wall as if punted. A bulldog-looking police officer in the starchy, white collared shirt of a supervisor stormed in. Their guest made a great deal of noise as he dragged a rickety wooden chair behind him on his way toward the holding tanks. He stopped at their cell, positioned the chair just outside of the bars, and sat, taking care with the gun belt holding up his sizeable gut.

The white shirt-wearing officer took to the sitting position like the old saying about ducks to water. He rocked back on the hind legs of the chair and folded his hands around his midsection. He took a deep breath and said, "How's it going gentleman? You enjoying your stay with us? I'm Chief Lawson, and I just wanted to ask you guys with some questions. Maybe see if we can get this craziness to make a little more sense."

The chief's large gut almost eclipsed everything else about him. With great effort, one could draw their attention from this Mount Fuji of a stomach and discover a piercing set of swimming pool blue eyes and a freshly groomed, salt-and-pepper tinged goatee.

"So to set our ducks in a row, can I make sure whom I'm speaking with?" Chief Lawson paused and brought a tired-looking notepad out of his shirt pocket. He flipped to the middle of the loose-leaf pad and spoke while reading. "Just like in grade school. I'll go through a roll call, but you don't have to say *here*. All I want from you two is to tell me if I get something wrong. I figure you boys can handle that. You both seem capable enough."

Conole situated himself so he faced the cell door. Meeting this Chief Lawson told him who had inspired the snake art in the cell. The drawing was all but identical to the high-ranking officer. "I've been here awhile and would like my phone call, please. Despite what you may believe, I am an American citizen, like my friend here. As such we're entitled to the same rights as everybody else. I'm also owed legal counsel, or do you intend to deny me this along with everything else?"

Chief Lawson tapped his notebook and grimaced at the interruption. "You've been booked, but you haven't been charged. Because of this, we can keep the two of you here for twenty-four hours before violating any constitutional rights. That is your free education on constitutional law."

Wadim growled and started to stand, but a small movement from the chief convinced him it would be better to stay seated. The chief's demeanor seemed calm, but beneath the surface, one could sense violent waters. Both Conole and Wadim had experience with folks pretending to be human. The Fogies could have given the chief notes on the performance. They sensed a great and violent storm brewed underneath Lawson's false mask of joviality; he was a person capable of great violence.

Wadim lowered his voice until it held none of its usual bite. "Look, I've told all this already to your-not-so-friendly-deputies. I'll repeat it again though for your benefit. You see, this year I've been having issues with insulin and blood sugar. Regrettably, I am still getting used to the symptoms. I mistook them for having a cold, and well…you know the rest."

The chief fiddled with a gold band on his finger and his body language read like a threat of danger. Beware bored and agitated; proceed at your own risk.

He once more tapped his notebook and said, "Could either of you tell me if breaking and entering are symptoms?"

Wadim dropped his head. "It's not unheard of."

Chief Lawson cracked his knuckles. "Suppose I believe this whole story about you selling stamps. I mean, since neither of you have a criminal record. Also, you weren't caught with any store property in your possession—at least none that we know about. You contaminated a crime scene and ruined any chance for gathering DNA. You understand this could help a killer go free when we make an arrest."

Conole's stuttered and stumbled to express himself. "That was unintentional, completely. We're truly sorry for the headache this may have caused. I have never been one to break the law willfully. Neither of us are part of the criminal element. In fact, we both support law enforcement and everything you guys do."

With a snort Wadim said, "Don't be taken in by him, Conole. This is all horse manure and scare tactics. They're not going to catch who killed that shopkeep. They're not even sure it was a man, going by what they did to the body. Go ahead and tell me I'm wrong."

Conole nudged his bunkmate and attempted to reign in Wadim's fury with a raised eyebrow. "Hey, there's no need to overexert yourself and end up sick again. Why, the chief here is only doing his job. He's being more than fair with his assessments. I mean, come on. He hasn't charged us yet. That's a good thing."

"Bah, they are demented if they believe the thing responsible will ever see the inside of a cell," Wadim replied with enough force that spit flew from his lips.

In an immediate response, Chief Lawson and all his extra weight rose. The chief, who no doubt loved sitting in any form, came purposefully to his feet. His rough hands found one another before the bars as if in prayer. "Mr. Stoica, funny, it doesn't say 'psychic' anywhere on your immigration papers. Please elaborate on what you think you know. In the report, the property owner indicates you had a lot to say about the Black Cloves. I would like to hear how they factor into all of this. Why don't you tell me everything you know about our murder victim or his killer and supposed secret societies?"

Conole didn't like where the conversation was going. He thought Wadim and the police chief were engaging in some weird cat-and-mouse game. The sort cops played all the time on bad police shows. Hadn't the man in the store mentioned this chief by name? Did that mean they were in cahoots? He hoped it was more small-town kinship and nothing sinister.

Conole chuckled nervously and said, "We were looking to become members is all. The idea was maybe the two of us could finagle an invite."

Wadim spat something dark and chunky into the corner of the cell, the color of which didn't look like anything a human body should produce. "You're wasting your time, Conole. I don't know much about secret societies, but I know they have ways to identify each other. Our hapless visitor here is a Clove, he's even wearing one of their decoder rings. He's playing games with us."

The chief's answering grin all but confirmed the accusation. He spun the plain gold band he had been playing with around to show the insignia of the incomplete leaf hiding on the other side. "You're a clever rascal, aren't you? What gave it away?"

Conole didn't know how Wadim came by this information, but he thought eating the ichor played a role in it. He wondered even more about what Wadim had seen in the blood.

Wadim feigned a tip of his imaginary hat. "The stranger in the shop wore a similar ring. I remember seeing it when he raised his silly club, but the gold of yours suggest a high rank. Take note, Conole, we're in the court of a chancellor, or at the very least an abbot."

Chief Lawson's cheerful demeanor dried up like the Mohave Desert. In the absence of humor, his face sagged. His jowls became more pronounced. "You certainly have an eye for little details. You would have been a decent cop, except you like to run your mouth." Chief Lawson's unprotected expression was one of disgust.

Conole no longer saw any reason for pretenses. "Regardless of who, someone in that store was dabbling with forces better left alone. I could see the black magic in the air. It was like a greasy film covering everything," he said.

Wadim frowned. "Please put this in your report. Whatever your real concerns may be, just know my short comrade here has a built-in detector when it comes to witchcraft and devilry. It makes me wonder how often your local parish has seen you in the pews. I bet not recently."

The chief kicked the bars hard enough to rattle the cell door. His cop voice came out like a secret weapon. The authority in his words added to his presence and commanded attention. "It's a gag, right? You tax-paying citizens talking about sorcery with straight faces. You break into a store and turn around and accuse the police of being part of the satanic panic?"

Wadim mocked the chief's official tone with his own. "Dear sir, it occurs to me that you're a Clove, and the late store owner was a Clove. Why doesn't that fall under a conflict of interest? I'm guessing you shouldn't even be in here interviewing us. Unless this isn't in any official capacity, and you've been lying since you sat down?"

Chief Lawson folded his notebook closed and shoved the chair back toward the end of the corridor. "I guess we're finished here. If you sit tight and be patient, you'll be out of that cell in a few hours, I'd say give or take. Consider this a charity on behalf of the Cloves, so we can't be too bad."

"That'd be great," Conole said. "We didn't do anything wrong. We're just two people in the wrong place and the wrong time. Let's forget all this talk of Cloves and magic."

Chief Lawson took his chair and headed toward the door, but Wadim had one more thing to say.

He put his mouth between the bars of the cell and yelled, "Hey, Officer Friendly? That gentleman at the antique shop, your friend with the shades? He told you to come talk to us, didn't he? What, you take orders from him, or is it the other way around?"

Chief Lawson opened the door, going into the outer offices with the clatter of ringing phones and buzzing radios rushing to fill the space. He looked back over his shoulder and shouted, "Mr. Stoica, we all answer to someone. Don't forget even the devils of hell have a pecking order."

In the wake of his reply, Chief Lawson left them to sit and wait.

Once they were alone again, Wadim sneered at the camera and rubbed his stomach. "My insides still haven't settled, but I didn't want that fellow to see any weakness. I don't trust him at all. You would do well to not believe anything they say. These police are wolves in sheep's clothing."

Conole stared at the snake drawing. "Might be better to say snakes. The things that crawl on their bellies."

"Speaking of bellies, my stomach churns, I fear a revolt is coming."

"I doubt a little more vomit is going to hurt the sink," Conole said.

Wadim patted Conole's shoulder and whispered, "Sorry, dear friend, but it's not wanting to travel through that end."

Chapter 9

Inside the police lobby, Pyles studied the bulletin board of wanted posters and flyers for missing dogs. He tried to keep himself distracted while Bronagh spoke with the officers working the front desk.

Pyles's overworked nose now recoiled at every scent. Every stench came in unfiltered and unprotected. He fought the nausea by sniffing his palms. Before entering the courthouse, he had rubbed in the smell of grass on his hands from the bit he found growing outside. The earthen aroma did wonders to settle his insides.

"What's the hold up?" Pyles asked from the bulletin board.

"Paper work," Bronagh replied as she started another round of verbal boxing with those sworn to protect and serve.

One of the deputies, with a scowl permanently etched into the bedrock of his face, stepped up with a clipboard. He flipped through the backlog of paperwork and said, "Yep, your friends are here, and it looks like they're going to be released within the hour. That's pending a small restitution fee and an informal ruling."

Bronagh clapped her hands at the good news. Had she the ability, she might have done a cartwheel. "A slap on the wrist? That is fantastic—you can believe me. They're not bad people. In fact, I don't believe they've even been ticketed for littering."

Pyles chuckled at the awkwardness of everything. He put a finger under his nose and wiped at eyes red with irritation. He kept expecting another spectral film screen to appear, one more phantom film to drive him completely insane.

He cleared a throat full of phlegm and said, "I'm glad they're alive and getting sprung, but I don't think I'm going to be able to stick around. The smell of this place is getting to me and maybe something else I can talk about later. It's too much weird for me to lay on you here and now. Let me get a firm handle on what it is first, and then I'll do a Q and A."

Bronagh let a single painful grimace slip by a preoccupied Pyles, who appeared more concerned with the exit. "Go get yourself together. I'll fetch Wadim and Conole, and we'll meet at my apartment and go from there. I'll let the boys know you were here, and they're in your thoughts."

Pyles nodded in appreciation. He clutched his truck keys and inched toward the door.

Bronagh watched as the sweat trickled down his weathered face and crept along the long broom like bristles of his beard. Something had obviously gotten under his skin, but still he'd said nothing.

Around them Deer Rose's finest answered calls and played grab ass like a bunch of drunken college kids on spring break. The dispatch radio fired off with calls about trespassing hunters, but the officers paid these things no mind.

Pyles took in the room's fragrance of cheap mouthwash and commodity disinfectant and did his best not to bolt into the fresh air. "I'm going to go ahead and hit the road. I mean, you got this anyway."

Pyles wasn't sure why, but he decided to give Bronagh a half hug before departing. He plunged his nose into the bouquet of her cinnamon skin and detected not for the first time the sour sweetness of illness. Once more, he said nothing of this, but stored it away for something else to worry about.

"Just say the word and I'll park it over there and wait with you. Just say it, old gal," Pyles whispered into her ear.

"It's not a big deal. Go collect your thoughts. I'll text you when we're free of this place," Bronagh said.

"Okay, well, tootles." Pyles covered his nose as if the air held poisonous vapors and fast walked out of the building.

Ten minutes later, the sound of shuffling feet on the smooth concrete floor announced Wadim and Conole's arrival. In his current state of calcified filth, Wadim resembled an unwashed street person and Conole seemed to painfully limp with every step.

At seeing her, Conole put forth the most labored smile. Bronagh took note of the way Wadim avoided her gaze as they went through their arraignment. She beheld no jury of peers nor any sort of impartial judge. An older man with a large gut and a white shirt seemed to have accepted the role of Lady Justice.

The man with the large sumo stomach opened the floor with an overly loud declaration, "I, Police Chief Lawson, a duly elected representative of Eller County, will preside over this informal hearing, a hearing as agreed upon by the absent owner of the property in question and of the accused perpetrators." The chief dramatically projected his voice and Bronagh suspected somehow the whole dog-and-pony show was being recorded.

The chief paused for effect before continuing. "The resolution has been discussed at length and agreed upon by all parties involved. The accused agree to enter a plea of no contest for a lighter judgment. This is correct, gentleman?"

That must have been Conole and Wadim's cue to chime in. They were too enamored with the chief's diction and the absurdity of the whole situation. Both stood there, silently nodding.

Conole stood as tall as he could and said, "That's correct, sir. I plead no contest."

"As do I," Wadim added, with his arms folded over his chest.

The chief nodded, his lips already moving before Wadim could finish his statement. "Very well, and under these conditions, I am prepared to render my verdict and commence with sentencing. I put forth a fine and restitution to be paid in full to the court at a cost of $186 per man. In addition, the defendants will be sentenced to eight hours of community service at the Lutheran Grace soup kitchen." The chief concluded the process by slapping the wooden divider with a gavel.

Bronagh joined the boys at the desk and patted each of them on the shoulder. She wanted to make sure they were fine and really leaving. Both Conole and Wadim favored her with a grin and went to gather their confiscated belongings from the police storage. Conole almost wept to have his cane back.

"Lads, I'm so glad you're all right," Bronagh said, not shy about her eyes watering. She touched each of them again in turn putting her finger against their shoulder to feel, for sure, they were safe.

Conole gave the tip of her finger a tiny peck of a kiss. "Safe my dear, and dearly wanting to be away from this snake's den."

Wadim's pale skin showed the first tinge of color at Bronagh's touch. He glanced around the office and said, "We survive, but what of the lummox?"

"He was here, but started feeling ill, his nose, I believe," Bronagh said.

Conole took a painful step to the exit. He examined his returned cellphone and cleared away numerous missed calls and messages. "I'll text him and let him know we're free and clear."

The Fogies left the station as quickly as their age would allow. Wadim cast a nervous glance behind them and muttered, "We have other concerns directly, like the thing those fools brought back to life. I dared not say anything inside, but I witnessed the man from the antique store's murder or at least part of it."

Conole, leaning heavily on the cane, stopped to peer back toward the police barracks. "I feared the Cloves were devil worshippers, and to make matters worse, they wear the uniforms of law enforcement."

Bronagh paused to make sure Conole didn't need a brief rest for his legs. Seeing the pain had abated, she said, "It's sordid business we best not concern ourselves with. I know you're disappointed, Wadim. We all are, but the universe is giving us a sign. We need to accept the end that comes for everyone."

Wadim found great reasons to stare at the gravel crunching under their feet. "I have failed the group once more. I tell you there are possibilities here. The Black Cloves used something to rouse a creature, dead body, back to life, some relic of power. That is what I felt that night in the woods."

When Wadim said "group," he turned to Bronagh. He stared at her for a moment before averting his gaze once more.

Bronagh guided them to her car and let the men situate themselves. Conole chose the passenger seat and Wadim ended up in the back. The two of them melted into the seat cushions as exhaustion overtook them.

"Seat belts, gentlemen. We don't want to encourage any more trouble with the law," Bronagh said.

She made it as far as pressing on the brake pedal before she felt the mysterious tingling. Like being accidently shocked by a loose wire, the sensation of the ether tore through her with the coolness of frozen tundra. The unexpected energy struck Conole and Wadim as well. The three Fogies became prisoners of the bitterly cold and paralyzing pleasure suddenly tip-toeing along every inch of skin.

The electrifying pulse of the other world filtered through them, the energy living beings were never meant to feel. Like a drug, it stirred up the receptors of both pleasure and pain. The ether came like a chill wind, prickling over flesh and raising the small hairs of the neck. The ether tickled them as a soft cool finger dancing along the spine till the sensation teetered on the unbearable.

Adrift in the sea of extreme intensities, the seconds became eons, and a single exhale went on like the endless cycle of the seasons. When the feeling finally subsided, the three came to like drunks stirred from a wild night of debauchery.

Bronagh collapsed against her door, opening it to find the fresh air her lungs screamed for. Her head swooned. She labored to form a thought other than expletives. "That was like a hundred haunted houses and a dozen séances," she said.

"I haven't experienced anything like that in a long time." Conole acted as if he wanted to say more, but a departing spasm halted him.

In a breathless rasp, Wadim said, "So who is ready to apologize for not believing me? Tell me you do not weep for more of that—the flirtation of death and immortality intertwined."

Bronagh labored for a calming breath. "My God, what caused that?"

Wadim wiped away a gob of snot and replied, "I have some ideas."

"That stuff, for a moment, I swear, I almost dematerialized. I almost became a spirit again," Conole said. "I want more of whatever it was, so long as it doesn't kill me."

Wadim smiled. "Finally, you have begun to speak my language."

Chapter 10

Pyles fled the police station as fast as he could. He planned on running until the air tasted better. Once he made it to the truck's driver seat, Pyles peeled away in a spray of gravel. The old truck frame shook and rattled from the stress, but its complaints fell on deaf ears. Pyles pressed harder on the gas pedal and pushed the ancient engine further than he normally dared.

Once safely beyond the city limits, he rolled the windows down and dropped back under the speed limit. With Deer Roses' stink diminishing, he imbibed the fresh breeze in full-throated, mouth-stretching gulps like someone gorging on air. These gulps cleaned something off his being a shower would never be able to touch. The fresh breeze temporarily refreshed him better than any cupful of expensive coffee.

The crisp wind revitalized him, but five or so miles shy of the first interstate onramp, the oily rotten, scent of something else filled the truck's interior—the unmistakable stink of the black goop from the sidewalk. The immediate eye watering and headache suggested a river of it flowed somewhere nearby.

He associated the mysterious goop with his strange vision. He didn't see how the two couldn't be related. Like most bloodhounds, once Pyles found a good trail, he wanted to follow it to the end. This was his obsession and one he tried to keep hidden away from the others. This desire sparked a curiosity he had to sate, consequences be damned.

Pyles did his best to guide the truck into a clear spot on the shoulder of the road. His curiosity drove him to kill the engine and investigate. For him to smell it like he had, the source had to be close.

"You're a dam fool if you get out of this truck," he said to himself. "But last time I got a whiff I had to sit through a bad movie. Seems like I shouldn't be driving anyway."

With the issue settled, he put two shaky legs on the road. He cracked his window and put an old bandana in the window so it would look like another broken- down truck by the side of the road. He hoped he'd be back before any vandals or tow trucks showed up.

Pyles tested his sniffer and picked out the strange odor like an invisible sewer line running over the hills. Pyles didn't put a whole lot of stock in the notion of fate, but coincidence seemed a halfhearted explanation to justify everything. With nothing else to go on other than a feeling in his stomach, he pursued the stink's source with his knife from under the seat at the ready.

Beyond the highway, the flat hilltop sloped away to a field garnished with weeds and a wall of briar bushes. All the thriving vegetation and the stretch of marshland beyond suggested an underground stream fed the land. An old four-wheeler trail kept Pyles's boots from the mud and let him cut across the field to the higher, dryer ground.

Even at this distance, he could still make out the sound of passing cars on the interstate. An air horn ripped through the trees, startling him. This little jump almost turned Pyles around. He wondered about the rationality of what he was doing, but it was as if something whispered to the possibilities of what lay beyond the next hill. Spurned forward by this need to know, he continued his pursuit.

On the other side of the swamp, Pyles walked for a quarter mile before he came to the ravaged remains of a tree stand. The heavy camouflaged canvas had been shredded like confetti. The broken supports carried a single long spray of the ichor like the markings of an animal claiming its territory. Something destructive had passed this way not very long ago.

Around him, the woods had gone silent except for the rustling of leaves. The countryside seemed to be holding its breath. Pyles noticed the shift as he approached a small hilltop not far away. His grip tightened on the knife.

At the hill's crest, he discovered the shriveled remains of a spotted doe empty of its insides. The blood-smeared carcass had almost been completely covered in black ichor and carried indentations of a hand strong enough to leave an imprint in thick tendons and sinew. Strange, deep, circular puncture wounds penetrated the corpse in a dozen different spots.

He figured the doe's remains had nothing more to tell him, but then Pyles spied the bullet hole in its shoulder. The lack of clotting around the wound said it couldn't have been more than a couple of hours old.

He put everything he had into sniffing beyond the ichor's stench for what lay underneath. The twinge of a headache made the task painful. He found the thinnest trace of gunpowder in the air and a taste of store-bought deer scent. Pyles focused on those like a fresh path and let his nose lead him further into the woods.

Another 500 yards of sniffing and he arrived at a large elm tree and the perfect scene for future nightmares. The tree's heavy boughs creaked with a suspended pair of mutilated corpses resembling human cutting boards.

The dead men's camouflage shirts dangled around their shredded faces, exposing bellies torn open from stem to stern. The would-be poacher's entrails were used to bind their feet to the tree like field-dressed animals abandoned to the wild. The corpses and surrounding area were dripping with an ichor still fresh enough it hadn't started disintegrating in the sun.

The intensity of the stink drove Pyles to smear an entire container's worth of honey-based lip balm from the truck under his nose. The scent of whatever had done the butchering lingered on for a few yards past the little horror show only to peter away to nothing. The trail ended just beyond the tree, and Pyles guessed he missed all the fun by less than an hour. Whatever the possible reasons for such a massacre escaped him, as did the reasons for the desecration to the remains.

The bloody ground held more of the antique boot prints from Conole's photo, but like the smell, they too disappeared a few feet past the bodies. This suggested the wearer had maybe taken flight or simply vanished.

An unexplained curiosity brought him to the dirt around the roots of the murder tree. Under the crime scene, a large section of the earth had been recently disturbed. Something about this struck him as odd. Pyles couldn't put a finger on why, but a strange urge to dig overtook him—almost a compulsion to see what lay beneath the soil. This was where the path had led him, and the best paths ended in treasure. Pyles seized upon this with blind certainty.

He squeezed around the dangling bodies, paying them almost no mind in this pseudo-trance. Pyles used the knife to break up the loose soil then plunged his hands into the crumbling soil. He didn't have to dig very deep before his fingers brushed something solid. Less than a foot down he came upon a velvet bag. The bag was slightly smaller than a potato sack, dirt stained, and faded from age. With a good yank he pulled it free, careful not to harm the contents. Whatever the bag held had the shape of a medium trash can.

He cradled the bulging bag in his arms and surrendered to the obsessive desire to know its secrets. The question of what it hid overtook every rational concern. He stepped behind the tree and with his back braced against the rough bark, Pyles peeled the bag away from its hard insides. The excitement had become a buzzing in his ear and the pounding of an overworked heart drowned everything else out.

He removed the bag to find a lead seal covering the top of what must have been a giant canning jar, the same type someone might use to display a science experiment in a museum. The physical change though didn't take place until his fingers happened to brush against the jar's sides. That's when the world turned in on itself.

He had intended to do nothing more than to wipe the glass clean. However, once the flesh of his fingers touched the strange jar, his muscles seized as if caught by a terrible cramp. An invisible door had been opened, and energy from the ether poured outward. More than he had ever felt. More than he had ever dreamed existed.

The energy funneled from the glass directly into Pyles. This caused the hairs along his arms to grow coarse and matted like an animal's. His bones popped and elongated as his body underwent an inhuman transformation. His jaw snapped open as it widened and stretched forward to make way for extra teeth.

Pyles dropped the jar and greeted the solid earth with his less-than-solid butt. He heard a pop in his spine as his bottom stuck the ground, and already he noticed the coarse hair vanishing like the rest of the changes. As if emerging from a dream, he reeled from what had seemed impossible.

The jar had tilted in the fall, but didn't break. Pyles considered this a blessing. He had recovered enough to see the demonic-looking fetus thing preserved inside the glass. Like a giant science experiment, the creature seemed to be someone's sick attempt at preserving a malformed newborn.

Breathlessly Pyles said, "That vision I saw—it was from you? You were calling to me, weren't you? You brought me here?"

Pyle's question went unanswered, but he didn't need a reply. He sensed the truth. He didn't dwell on what had happened there or what had buried the jar and left. These were questions for another time, a concern for the future Pyles to worry about. Instead, he concentrated on the pulse that traveled up his nervous system every time his flesh met the jar. With each caress, more ether flooded the woods and the jar directed this energy directly into him.

The moment his skin made contact Pyles's human form began once more to shift into something not quite beast or man. Unable to do anything else, he shouted, which soon became a

wolfish howl. The man vanished beneath the long dormant
wolf.

Chapter 11

Bronagh went ahead of Conole and Wadim into the living complex. Both men knew the routine and signed in as visitors. The lobby bustled with residents reading the newspaper and crocheting clothes too ugly and tiny to be for anything other than a pet. The air smelled of sanitizing cleaner and muscle rub. The television in the day room played an old detective show on full volume. The program's opening siren blared like an air raid.

"This place never fails to surprise me," Wadim said with a sneer, his disdain rousing him better than any medicine could.

Conole used the wall like a second walking stick. "It's good you can still find surprises in life."

"I did not mean this as a good thing." Wadim passed by a man with a similar hairstyle, and they exchanged uncomfortable nods. "Most assuredly not a good thing."

Bronagh focused on the miracle of getting to her apartment without any of the committee members seeing them. The incident in the car left the Fogies reeling, and they dared not speak of it. At least not yet, not before being somewhere safe from prying eyes and ears.

Bronagh yawned and said, "Wadim, you're the most negative person I know."

Wadim twirled his fingers. "If you want positive, check your battery terminals. What I saw orchestrated by the Cloves does not inspire happy smiling feelings. We are fortunate we made it out of that snake's den in the first place. Then that business in their parking lot. I ache to hear what you make of it."

Conole paused to deliver a one-handed massage to his cramping thigh. "It was foolish to put that gunk in your mouth; you could have killed yourself. I hope it was worth it."

Wadim's retort came in a poor imitation of Conole's accent. "We see that you threw up all over your nice, new shirt. We see you almost died so we could maybe escape this abysmal old age. Gee, thank you from the bottom of our collective hearts. Death lingers just over the shoulder, but we don't worry about that, do we?"

The elevator opened and the Fogies entered in a single file. There wasn't much to say, but Conole touched his belly and whispered, "I hope this elevator goes quick because I feel a toot of flatulence coming on. Whew, I think it's going to be a bad one, too."

"Don't you dare," Bronagh chuckled.

"Did your manners fail to abscond when we did?" Wadim pressed the button for Bronagh's floor dozens of times.

Conole fought the good fight and held off the flatulence. At the *ding* of her floor, they came around the corner in a rush, and Wadim, not paying attention to his surroundings, almost bulled someone over.

This proved the universe did indeed like to punish liars, because that someone turned out to be an already angry-looking Bonnie Sweeten.

Bronagh tried to intervene, but the shouting had already begun. Bonnie and Wadim both shared the unique ability to instantly escalate any situation.

Bonnie pointed out a stray thread on her sweater sleeve. She tugged on the loose thread until the sewing came undone. "Look here, you ruined it. Why don't you watch where you're going? There are handicapped residents that use this hallway. They don't need a rabid, stinky, moose stomping all over them. I or someone else could have been seriously hurt."

Wadim started to raise his voice. He matched hard stares with Bonnie and a moment later he cast his eyes elsewhere. "A rabid moose? Dear lady, this does not warrant name-calling. If it makes a difference, I am not currently in full capacities, either. Consider me like one your impaired neighbors."

Bonnie's eyes narrowed as she surmised their group. "Well, I should have known this was one of your guests, Bronagh. I trust these friends of yours signed in downstairs. Or maybe the rules don't apply to you? This is exactly why I want a closer watch on who comes and goes here."

Bronagh flinched against the woman's rage. "I apologize. We just left the emergency room. He must still be a tad foggy because of the medication. You're not hurt, are you? I can ring one of the nurses if you need to be looked at."

Bonnie stared at the arm in which Wadim had bumped her. She looked at it as if her eyes could X-ray through the fabric all the way to the bone. "I don't need your help for anything. It's probably going to bruise. I have a vitamin deficiency and need to be careful, but as I tell my doctors all the time, I can't account for everyone else out there. I'm going to file a complaint over this."

"Naturally," Bronagh said. "You do what you must to ease the pain."

Bronagh put Conole in a single file line behind Wadim and together they squeezed against the wall. This gave the remainder of the hallway over to Bonnie.

Bronagh swept her arm to show Bonnie she had the right of way. "A cold compress could help, maybe some ibuprofen. You should tend to it before the skin raises."

Under Bronagh's direction, the Fogies started off, but Bonnie Sweeten still had more to say. She remained in the hall and shouted after them, "I figure you should hear it from me before anyone else. It seems some of the folks you invited to your secret meeting thought it would be better if I also attended. Then, surprise, surprise, the meeting didn't happen. Tell me— should I take it personally?"

This stung Bronagh, but she refused to show it.

Several minutes later, she welcomed the other Fogies into her home. Conole shuffled to the bathroom, offering condolences about any smell. Wadim went to the computer desk and eased into the chair. He groaned and covered his face when Bronagh brought over aspirin and a bottle of water. He took several of the pills with most of the water while he observed the condition of his hair in her computer monitor.

"When he's done defiling your bathroom perhaps could I trouble you for a shower and a clean towel? This stuff is really beginning to stink, and I'd like to get it off my skin."

Bronagh put a kettle on the stove for a fresh cup of tea and set out three mismatched mugs collected over her years of travel. From the other room, she watched Wadim cough something into her wastebasket. He wiped a sleeve across his chin and slouched further into the chair.

Bronagh perused the different teas and called out, "I still have a few of Michael's outfits. If you want, I can lend you a set of pajamas while I wash your clothes."

Wadim peeked at her through half eyelids as he began to doze. "I cannot see any of your late husband's clothes fitting me with any kind of comfort."

"There are some jogging pants and a sweater that may do the job."

"Are you sure you'd be fine with me wearing them?" Wadim asked.

Bronagh grinned and moved through the different teas like going through names in a Rolodex. "It would do me good to see someone in his old things. It will remind me of the old days."

The toilet flushed, and Wadim began to snore. A minute later, a bashful Conole joined Bronagh in the kitchen. He had scrubbed his face hard enough his cheeks flushed red.

"If that's tea, you truly are a gift from the heavens. I'm afraid I'm going to require sugar and lots of it," Conole said with a yawn and a stretch. "Perhaps a dollop of cream, too, if you have it."

"Check the fridge," Bronagh said. "My, he is sawing logs in there."

Conole found the creamer and piled it into his mug. "He almost died. Wadim should probably be in a hospital bed."

Over cups of good caffeine-enriched tea, Conole retold the events of the antique store. He placed careful emphasis on the stranger, the Cloves, and Wadim's seizure. Bronagh held the mug and listened wide-eyed as the odder details of the story emerged.

When Conole finally fell silent she said, "I was going to offer to heat up a casserole I had made, but I'm not sure if I could eat anything after hearing that."

Conole allowed the steam from his teacup to clear his sinuses of everything left over from the damp jail. It warmed his bones and a lot of the aches in his legs fell silent for the moment. "Sorry I know it doesn't exactly cause the taste buds to tingle, but if you're offering, it might do us all some good to have a bite."

They heard Wadim cry from the other room in a half-sleep. His twitching legs kicked at the bottom of the desk. He swatted at imaginary assailants until he rolled off the chair and came awake on the carpeted floor of Bronagh's apartment.

Wadim fixed a loose hair and said, "Ugh, that ichor will not leave me be. It continues to show me things. I need to flush it out of my system, but I'm not sure how to do it." He covered his mouth and ran to the kitchen sink just before vomiting up the pills and water.

"I'd hold off on the casserole," Conole said. "I lost my appetite."

Wadim found the third untouched mug of tea and gargled with a warm mouthful before spitting the contents into the sink. Both Conole and Bronagh saw the brackish quality to the saliva. Wadim refilled his cup from the kettle, this time going heavy with the honey.

"Try some cinnamon; it may help settle your stomach," Bronagh said.

"It's also good for the blood sugar," Conole added.

Wadim took the advice and added a teaspoon out of a plastic shaker. Once full to the brim, he carried his mug to the couch. Conole followed and navigated to the other side of the cushion. Bronagh allowed the boys to get comfortable before she chose the now vacated computer chair.

Wadim's stomach produced a gurgle, and he let out a long burp. He waved away the smell and said, "Would someone like to speak on the strength of the ether from the parking lot? You cannot deny that indeed something powerful is at work, although I fear it has to do with whatever killed the shopkeeper."

Conole shuddered at the mention of the experience in the car. "You were right, Wadim. I've never felt anything like it since being human. I wouldn't have said it was impossible to come that close to the other side and not pass over."

A grinning Wadim wiped his lips and said, "Me, too, but it is an avenue we will have to ignore. It is a tease and nothing more."

Wadim picked at a scraping of the dried ichor under his nail that had escaped his earlier tasting. Seeing this, Conole offered him a tissue. With a laugh, Wadim took it and a squirt of sanitizer from Bronagh.

He sensed the others watching him and said, "You can relax. I'm officially back on the wagon as far blood goes. Take this as me going cold turkey for the remainder of my life."

Conole also had a squirt of sanitizer and replied, "It does me good to hear you say this, but mate, I have a lot of questions. Like namely, what possessed you to act on such an impulse? You could have died, and then where would that have left me?"

Wadim sneered, "I'm sorry my death would have inconvenienced you." He grabbed a pad of paper and a pen off the counter and went back to lounging. "I know you have more questions. I need to organize everything in my head first. Everything came in a jumbled rush. I'm already having a hard time remembering what I saw. It was indeed the blood of the shopkeep I tasted, but also something else. Something like blood, but different, older, more unnatural."

Bronagh put her empty cup down and went for the flask. "Wadim, the offer still stands to shower if you would like more time get your mind right."

Wadim shook his head and said, "I want to tell you what I saw first. Why don't you busy yourself by checking the site and tell us if there's anything there?"

He began to scribble through the ordeal on paper like a drunk attempting to retrace the steps of an embarrassing night. His penmanship drizzled onto the crisp sheets like frosting being hastily squeezed onto a cake.

Bronagh supervised for a moment before she turned the computer on. Wadim reached the end of the page and flipped it over to the clean backside. His scrawling lost all structure as partial ideas ran along the margins in no real order.

Conole's phone *dinged* with a text, and he paraphrased the message for them. "It's from Pyles. He's making sure we're all here and wants me to tell you guys to sit tight and not go anywhere."

Wadim shook his overworked writing hand and wiggled the cramps out of his bony fingers. "I'm almost ready. Pyles will have to get the abridged version when he gets here. This isn't something a sensible man does twice."

Conole put his phone away and said, "I guess I'll have to pay attention then."

Wadim tore his notes out and slapped the notebook down on the coffee table. "It's time, so allow me to tell you what I know of—what I beheld in the ichor and blood. There is something on the lose something these small-town Satanists awoke. However, this monster—this thing—those fools brought back to life. It won't change any of us. I apologize if you got your hopes up. It's an abomination of black magic and alchemy constructed to serve the darkest purposes. The dead shop owner's blood showed me much, but the other things in the blood weren't like anything I've ever tasted before."

Conole's mouth fell open and he whispered. "Wait, you mean that *stuff* was something's blood?"

Wadim nodded. "I have an idea it uses fresh blood to rejuvenate the stuff in its veins, almost like dialysis. The Cloves brought this dormant monstrosity over from a German bunker and figured it would be a cinch to reanimate and control. This Third Reich zombie proved to be more than their friend the shopkeeper could handle. This mistake cost him his life."

Bronagh opened a saved search page on the computer, typed in the key points of what Wadim described, and clicked *find*. "I've never heard of such a thing. I hope these foolish men didn't awaken something to end the world."

"In the shop, while you were convulsing, you said something about a fetus. What did you mean?" Conole asked.

"I don't remember, but it was something to do with that broken chest we found and its contents. I have a theory this pertains to the magic totem or charm they used to awaken the zombie. It puts out ether like nothing we have ever seen before," Wadim said.

Bronagh divided her interest between her friends on the couch and the computer, skimming over the search results in a crapshoot for something pertinent.

Wadim watched the computer from over Bronagh's shoulder and said, "I'll be surprised if there's anything online but try typing in 'German resurrection experiment.' In this thing's memories, I saw bunkers and Allied planes circling overhead and scared scientist welding metal to bones. They were praying to a god not found in any bible verse and begging for the same thing we seek, life after death."

Bronagh typed as instructed and said, "I for one don't have to hear anymore. We should remove ourselves from the situation in Deer Rose, whatever it may be."

Conole shifted his legs with a grimace. "I'm worried they're going to come after us. They may see our group as a threat. We all but taunted them in the cell."

Wadim went to the window and peered at the parking lot. "They might do a poor man's job of spying, but our little sect of Cloves have other things to worry about. This German zombie they reanimated is part of the equation. There's also the powerful talisman it took when it broke free. This talisman had enough juice to rouse the dead and who knows what else. This talisman is like a battery and their little walking corpse has it now."

Conole's phone *dinged* with a text. He read it and said, "Humans and magic never ends well, but a talisman can be a serious thing in the wrong hands. Pyles is on his way up and he says to make sure the blinds are closed."

"What for?" Bronagh asked.

Wadim crumpled his notes up and dropped them into the trash basket by the end of the couch. "Our friend has perhaps joined the health craze and is concerned with melanoma."

Bronagh scrolled through several computer pages. She gasped at an online thread of supposed ex-members of the Black Cloves. She paraphrased what she found out loud. "They deal in human sacrifices, occult paraphernalia, and believe chaos guides the universe. The higher-level members are reportedly told the truth. It isn't the Black Cloves as in clover, but Black Cloves as in the devil's hooves, cloven hooves."

Conole replied, "Cloven hoof, wow, it makes total sense when you say it. These aren't meddlers in the occult, but fully immersed devil worshippers."

Bronagh continued to scroll through pages, describing the demonic activity of secret societies and said, "I didn't get a great impression at the police station, but they hardly struck me as the demonic, zombie raising types. Incompetent and heavy-handed sure, but not evil."

Wadim gazed at the screen and muttered, "Bronagh, you and Conole have lived pretty good lives as humans; you've both seen and done much. Unfortunately for you, you came into the game late and were already adults. You missed the formative years where the seeds of evil are often planted through neglect, abuse, and cruelty. Even the gentlest soul can possess a speck of hate that needs nothing more than opportunity to grow. Give a person enough power and enough freedom and this speck can become their entire being."

"Rather cynical, aren't we?" a texting Conole mumbled. "Pyles says to unlock the door."

"Call me cynical if you want, but give that sweater woman from the hall power over who lives and dies. Do that and we shall finish this discussion," Wadim replied.

Bronagh went to the door and turned the latch before putting another kettle of tea on the stove. None of them were ready when Pyles charged in with his arms filled. He closed the door by mule-kicking it and bulldozed his way over to the kitchen counter.

He moved like a man dodging bullet fire, but never strayed far from the bulky cloth-wrapped shape he deposited on the Formica countertop. The thing had the circular form of a large pitcher, but a camouflage rag, and a dirt-smeared black velvet sack kept it a secret only the tall mountain man knew.

Bronagh had to take a step back to keep from being knocked over in the one-man stampede. She locked the door behind Pyles and said, "Have you taken an absence of your senses? Tell me you didn't make a scene by coming through the building like that."

Huffing and puffing Pyles said, "Nothing you'll have to worry about."

Conole said, "What do you have there?"

"This," Pyles answered.

In a grand flourish, Pyles tossed the camouflage rag into the corner, not noticing the smear of blood it left on the white walls. With howl of triumph, he ripped the black fabric away and Conole, Wadim, and Bronagh gasped at what lay underneath.

"That's a bloody fake," Conole said, forgetting about his leg pain as he shimmied off the couch to get a better look.

"Where did you find it?" Wadim asked. "I…I have seen it before only in dream."

Pyles sniffed and tapped his nose. "I smelled it out there in the woods. Darn thing was buried under a tree. Crazy, but it's like it kept tugging at me to find it."

Conole whispered, "Considering everything we've experienced recently, that doesn't sound crazy at all."

Wadim led with his face, so his eyes were level with the small, mummified body inside the glass jar. He imitated the head movement of a boxer slipping his chin over each shoulder to get a closer look at the preserved oddity. His mouth opened and hung there as if on a broken hinge.

The thick glass held a small, mummified corpse of a deformed infant. This specimen had a narrow skull containing two knobby horn-like points, above a deformed set of inhumanly large eye sockets. The rest of its monstrous-looking features were hidden behind its slender vine-like fingers as the thing lay in the fetal position. Unbelievably a forked tail dangled between curled up legs and bat-like wings.

"It looks like a haunted house decoration or a creepy Mexican piñata," Bronagh said. She fell into a loop of putting a finger up to the glass, but stopping short of contact.

"No one touch it, okay?" Pyles said. He used the black bag like an oven mitt to move the jar away from the edge of the counter. "This isn't a joke at you, Conole, but we have found the gold at the end of the rainbow."

Wadim circled like a shark transfixed by the strangeness of the glass's insides. "This is dire indeed. I know this thing, from the old man's blood. This preserved corpse is what helped the Cloves wake the dead. We need to get rid of it. Throw it over the New River Gorge and forget about it, or better yet, bury the damn thing."

Pyles laughed. "You're going to eat those words once you see this. Wadim, you were right about our chance finally coming."

Pyles put a single finger up to the glass and in response the hair on his arm rippled, thickened, and turned coarse like horsehide. The tendons and muscles swelled into thick powerful knots. In less than a second, the shaggy gray-brown hair of his head had grown to reach his shoulder and the bottom of a widening neck.

Into the tiny kitchen seeped an avalanche of energy and while Wadim, Conole, and Bronagh shuddered in its wake, the demonstration continued. Pyles now resembled a terrible half-man caught between different stages of the evolutionary ladder. His grip on the glass never faltered, and he hooked the still human elbow around the side of the jar.

Conole watched the claws spring from his friend's fingers and said, "Pyles what are you doing? Stop it—you can't turn into a wolf in the middle of an old folks' home."

In the wave of sensations Bronagh experienced, a moment where the veil between worlds thinned and revealed the specter of death lingering in the air. The dark specter possessed a gaping mouth poised to swallow them, but before she could discern more, the energy faded.

Pyles pushed the jar away with the last of his humanity. The instant his flesh ceased contact with the glass, the wolf overtaking him dissipated like smoke and the ebb of energy vanished.

The thing within the jar never stirred. It remained dead and preserved like a hunter's stuffed trophy.

Bronagh couldn't get the shadow of death out of her head. She had seen an ill omen and a prediction for a dark future. She sensed the jar at the center of it. She pursed her lips and said, "Get that demonic token or whatever it is out of my apartment."

Conole spied a droplet of red on the living room carpet and traced it to the camouflage rag. "Hell would be my guess. There was a taint to that energy I don't want to feel again."

Pyles wiped the excited slobber off his jaw and said, "You saw what it did for me. It can do the same for you—just touch the glass. Touch it, and the from what I've seen, so long as you keep contact, you can kiss this mortal coil good-bye."

Conole used the coffee table as a handrail and walked himself over to confront a smiling Pyles. "Have you asked yourself what's causing the change? It looks like a baby demon in there and meddling in dark magics always ends in disaster."

Pyles slid a fingernail down the glass and stopped before the change could move past his arm. "It's everything we ever wanted. It's power like you wouldn't believe. I don't want to call it fate, but there's no other word for it. This thing called to me, maybe to all of us."

Bronagh winced away from the jar. She dropped a dish towel over the top of the glass so she wouldn't have to look at it. She crept back as if the thing inside might break free and come flying after her. "We don't know any of the consequences this this may bring. There can be terrible ramifications we need to consider."

"The ramifications are on the bloody rag he tossed aside. The rag has a collar because it was someone's shirt," Conole said, joining Bronagh in a unified disgust.

"Oh, what did you do?" Bronagh asked.

Pyles picked up the remains of the shirt and dropped it in the wastebasket. "Cool your jets, the guy who went inside this was dead before I cut it off him. Whatever thing did the killing possessed enough sense to burry this jar underneath the bodies. Why it was buried, I don't know."

"The zombie," Wadim said.

"Zombie? What are you babbling about? I can tell you it wasn't any shuffling corpse that shredded two stout, well-armed men like kindling," Pyles replied.

"I better tell him," Wadim muttered. He gave a shortened version of his vision in the store, emphasizing the Satanic nature of the Cloves. Conole joined in adding details where he could.

Pyles looked at them through the glass and nodded. "Great story, but you need to try this thing. Come on—who's next? I know someone wants to flirt with the other side. I tell you, afterward you'll feel years younger."

Wadim couldn't avoid staring into the jar, "Are there any aftereffects? Do you believe it will do the same for us? Perhaps it is connected somehow to the wolf you once were. I don't yearn to sprout hair and worry about fleas."

"Touch it for a second, and then tell me to get rid of it," Pyles said, moving the towel away from the lid.

Bronagh returned to the computer searches and waited while the small hourglass icon said results were forthcoming. "No one has any answers. It's a guessing game. Don't pretend as if you know."

This caused Pyles's nostrils to flare. "I got an idea it works on desires, real desires. In the truck, I tried thinking of other things, but it was the wolf every time I touched it. I figure because way down inside, that's all I really want. Well, that and to go back in time 50 years, but I figure that's beyond this thing's powers. But then again, maybe not."

Wadim glanced at Bronagh. "I've made up my mind. I have weighed the risks and decided to try it. With the permission of the homeowner, I'll do a second, so we'll have a better idea of what this thing can do. Of what its purpose is."

Bronagh shook her head. "No one else is touching that thing while it's here. You want to do that, we're taking it somewhere else. I don't like it; the thing gives me the creeps. Makes my skin crawl."

Conole leaned to the side to see if he could perceive anything else of the creature from a different angle. "I agree with Wadim. We'll have to decide what to do with it eventually, but I want to know more before we make any decisions."

Wadim went into the kitchen and returned with a pair of oven mitts. "Fine, we need somewhere secluded, someplace out of the way. I suggest this county's little league field. I know it's outside of town. My nephew's son played T-ball there. I believe their season hasn't started. We should have the place to ourselves, and it's removed from any houses. We can take it there for an experiment. I have so many questions."

"Take the mitts," Bronagh said, "anything to get that thing out of my apartment. It's giving me the willies. I swear I can feel it staring at me."

"It's just your imagination," Pyles said. "Liberals tell me the same thing about the barrel of a gun. Powerful things make people nervous, and former banshee or not, your overly emotional human side is no different. One touch and you would see it's a gift."

Something scratched at the apartment door ending the discussion and causing the trio of men to gawk at Bronagh. She brought her lips together in a *shushing* gesture and the Fogies tensed. The scratching came a second time, and they waited in silence. It sounded like a cat wanting to be let in.

"Take that thing to the bathroom and close the door," Bronagh said.

Wadim and Pyles each put a hand on the towel covered jar. They grimaced at one another like dogs fighting over a soup bone.

"I got this," Pyles said.

"You've already had your turn. Don't be greedy; it's a sign of poor character," Wadim retorted. "I'm covered in vomit. Who do you think will draw the most attention?"

The pair would have stood there arguing, but Bronagh settled the debate for them. "Wadim is right. Let him take the thing, and Pyles, you join Conole on the couch. Please, everyone, try to look sane."

Pyles kept a palm on the jar's lid. Wadim sneered at the larger man, and they came nose-to-chin over the kitchen counter.

"Being that close you may as well kiss," Conole said. He made a smooching sound to emphasize how silly they were acting.

This joke poked holes in their bravado and a sullen Pyles went to the couch. Wadim pranced triumphantly and used the oven mitts to carry the towel-covered jar out of the room. He made sure to pause at the corner of the hall and smile for those still sulking.

Bronagh crept over to the door's peephole and looked out at Lita's cackling face.

Lita called through the door, "Bronagh, Bronagh, dear, are you in there? Bee-Ronagh, I thought I'd chat you up for a moo-moment, eh? Did you hear me say moo-moment, funny wasn't it?"

"She sounds drunk. Let me make sure she's okay." Bronagh turned the lock and Lita tumbled into the room in a fit of giggles. With the apartment door open, the rest of the building sounded alive with music, laughter, and someone screaming. Bronagh brought the other woman inside and shut the door just as someone yelled about a missing cat.

"Has everyone lost their mind?" Bronagh said as the cackling Lita attempted to crawl across the kitchen floor.

She waved at Pyles and Conole, and in the high whisper of a drunk muttered, "Your friend is so short. He's like a baby—it's the funniest thing. Do you figure he would let me swaddle him? Would you like that? Do you want to be swaddled like a baby?"

"Love, are you sure you didn't maybe have a drink or two too many at the meeting? I should probably help her back to her place and see that she gets to bed," Bronagh said.

She motioned for Conole and Pyles to stay there, and they both looked dumbfounded at this development. Lita came to her feet with Bronagh's help, and together they walked in tandem to the hall. In the corridor, both women were almost knocked over by a naked man running the floors. The nude jogger shook his privates as he headed in the direction of the stairs.

Further into the chaos, the Helmick sisters were using condiments to doodle on the wall. The project appeared to be a heard of ketchup dinosaurs racing towards a mustard yellow sun.

Lita's head had sagged until all the excitement perked her back up, and she muttered, "Don't you love how lively it is? I hate to tell you this, but Emperor Bonnie knew all about the meeting."

"I know, Bonnie told me," Bronagh said as they came to Lita's door. She thanked the stars that it happened to be unlocked. She didn't have the strength to steady her friend and root around in her purse for keys.

"Bronagh, I had the oddest tingling along my spine a little while ago. Then it was like I was sleepwalking. Isn't that odd? Maybe it was the tuna fish I had."

"Maybe everyone is doing a bit of sleepwalking," Bronagh answered.

She put an exhausted Lita to bed and was on her way back to the apartment when the flesh of her arm prickled over. Her heart fluttered, and she raced back to find Conole and Pyles staring at the bathroom.

The lights were off in hall, but they heard Wadim's mad laughter piercing the darkness. He emerged from the shadows with the uncovered jar held against his bare chest. His eyes glowed a terrifying red, and his feet seemed to float along the carpet.

"No, Wadim. What were you thinking?" Bronagh said.

The vampiric Wadim cracked his neck and pointed with a long, claw like nail. "Bronagh, Pyles was correct. It's the other side, and it's right here for us. I feel it, and I'm willing to try to bring each one of you across." He took a step and the shadows moved with him as if Wadim held dominion over the gloom.

Bronagh, Conole, and Pyles fled into the light of the living room as Wadim stalked them like the slow-moving monster of a nightmare. His usually heavy body glided along the carpet with the grace of a ballet dancer.

"Who's first?" Wadim whispered. "I'll change you, and when I put this thing down, you can do the same for me. Let's not be timid, I can make it a gentle process."

The other Fogies reached the wall by the couch and realized the retreat had run its course. Pyles raised a fist and Bronagh pulled a thick dictionary off the shelf and raised it overhead.

"Come on, don't make this any harder than it must be. The pain will be brief. A moment of discomfort before we'll all go together into the beautiful, endless dark," Wadim said.

Pyles looked to Bronagh and Conole for guidance. "I'll pass but thanks, anyway."

Bronagh pulled the computer chair over like a temporary barrier. "We don't know if this change would be permanent. What you're suggesting is a good recipe to end with three corpses. You need to snap out of it," she said.

Wadim's lips salivated with blood lust, but Bronagh's logic put an uncertain furrow in his brow. She used the second to fetch a grip on the pull string of the window's binds behind her. She hoped for the best and yanked them open, bathing the room in sunlight. The light eliminated the shadows and sent Wadim shrieking away, the jar slipping from his grasp.

Conole, forgotten on the sidelines, lurched forward and caught the falling jar in a bear hug. The contact of his bare skin against the glass caused a torrent of energy to surge out. Instantaneously, his entire body flickered between existence and nothingness. The glass floated to the ground as the flickering Conole shifted between dimensions, a living paradox, being both there and not there at the same time.

Bronagh shrieked and called his name. A long, agonizing second later, Conole's form solidified near the jar where they had last seen him. He looked disoriented and took a brief inventory of his various parts.

"I was there," Conole whimpered while he reached for the jar, now sitting uncovered on the floor. When his legs wouldn't support him, Conole crawled on his belly toward the glass.

Bronagh snatched a comforter off the couch and covered the thing before Conole could reach it. She put a foot on either side of the blanket and commanded the others to back away.

"Don't anyone of you move, or so help me, I'll jam my finger in your eye," she said.

Conole moaned, Pyles grinned, and Wadim lingered in the shadows.

From the hallway, Wadim peeked out and said, "Maybe you were right about that thing's effects. What do you think we should do?"

"I don't know," Bronagh replied, feeling a clench in her stomach. "I just don't know."

Chapter 12

The Fogies made it the little league field with no problems. The site wouldn't be open for several more weeks, but the volunteers had been working on getting it ready. The field sat several miles off the main road, all but hidden from the casual passerby. Hills dimpled the horizon, and a far-off cell tower flashed the occasional red light. The field had neighbors and no traffic, so there was no worry about the occasional fly ball.

The Fogies came in the same car and parked in the gravel lot. Wadim drove and made a grand production of backing in. Afterward they had a brief look around to make the place was really all theirs.

The field had been made game ready, but the season hadn't begun yet. The sod had the unnatural green of Astroturf and appeared well tended. The volunteers had indeed been working hard. The chain link fence carried billboards for the sponsors and the bright coloring of their logos almost glowed in the sun.

Bronagh figured since Pyles found the demonic jar buried in the ground, perhaps the dirt could keep its powers in check. At least hidden away, she hoped the thing couldn't do much harm. It still gave her the creeps, and she knew the earlier image of death she glimpsed somehow involved the jar.

She made her plans known and received no argument to the contrary. The park's supply shed didn't have a lock, and Conole volunteered to look for a shovel and some sod if available. His time on the other side, courtesy of the jar, had seemingly cured his leg pain and even added a bit of a spring to his step.

Wadim and Pyles put their hands on top of one another in a rush to unload their cargo. They compromised by sharing the weight in a split grip of Pyles going high, Wadim palming the bottom, and each holding a section of the blanket supporting the glass jar.

Conole paused in his task and said, "I've been pondering why the zombie even stole the jar from the Cloves in the first place. What purpose is there in taking the thing and burying it?"

In the freedom of the open space, Wadim shared his thoughts with a shout. "It's a mindless monstrosity being driven by demonic influence. Who can really say?"

The shed door didn't sit perfectly against the jamb, so Conole had to use his body weight to pull it open. "You say that, but mindless things don't safely walk an oversized glass beaker several miles. It makes me wonder what it may have been up to. It's not going to come looking for this thing, is it?"

"One dilemma at a time," Bronagh said. She covered her mouth and nose against the stinging wind coming off the distant mountains.

"I think it's this fetus or whatever it is," Pyles shouted over the sudden roar of the breeze as it filtered through the chain link fence and rattled the metal of the broken links. "I saw something earlier I can't explain. It makes sense to say this thing in the glass is the cause. The energy Wadim felt the night of the murder could have been it trying to contact anyone open enough to sense it."

Wadim scowled. "The hillbilly may be on to something here. Our small preserved fifth member might not be as dormant as we believed. Could be it pulling us and the zombie along some unknown path, and maybe the Cloves, too."

A lone popcorn wrapper, caught in the fence from seasons past, swirled free in the updraft and circled overhead before the air took it away. They all watched it go and turned to the blanket-covered jar, as if it was a living thing eavesdropping on the procession.

Wadim broke the mood with a prolonged cough. "Okay Boss, where are we burying our treasure? Should I be ready to paint the *X* of a treasure map on the ground?"

Bronagh studied the field. She considered underneath the bleachers, but happened on another spot. "Over there by the pitcher's mound. No one will notice the disturbed earth. I only wish we could bury it with a dump truck. I don't know how, but it affected the residents of my complex. You heard them—it's like they were teenagers again. It was unnerving and dangerous.

I don't like what that jar causes to happen to people. It's dangerous."

"Interesting choice of hiding places," Pyles replied. "I'm surprised you would let it anywhere near where kids hang out."

"We'll move it before the first game, but for the moment, I'll feel better knowing it's out here."

Conole found a small spade and brought it back. He shook his head about the sod. "I didn't see any in there. I'm not sure we really need it, though."

With the Bronagh leading the way, they carried the jar onto the field like a procession of mourners. Together, Pyles and Wadim lowered the jar onto the mound. They took up opposing positions around the glass as if guarding from an expected escape. Conole kicked the dirt and mulch of the pitcher's mound loose and took the first spade full of earth out.

Bronagh panted in the heat, and seeing this, Wadim said, "My dear, you haven't experienced its blessing like the rest of us have. We felt the raw ether and tell me we don't look all the better because of it. I've ceased vomiting while Conole is ready to long jump to the outfield. This miracle can be yours I truly believe with a single touch."

"I don't need any further temptation," Bronagh replied. "Can we hurry this along, please? I'd like this to be done and over with before the stars come out."

Pyles scoffed. "What are you talking about? That's not for a couple of hours yet. We have the time, and I wouldn't mind another go while there's a dollop of natural light left."

"Too damn much sun," Wadim growled. "It's not fair we're leaving at dark."

Pyles grimaced. "After what you pulled, it's probably safer for all of us."

Bronagh positioned herself as a barrier between them and the jar. "Don't describe it as a go—it's not a carnival ride. This is as dangerous as any weapon used in war. The allure is what scares me the most. You three are chomping at the bit to dally with it again. I don't like that."

"Come on, Bronagh, it may do something about the stuff eating up your insides," Pyles whispered.

His tone was low, but she heard him as if he had shouted from the rooftops. So did Conole and Wadim, whose lack of a reaction said this came as no surprise. Bronagh couldn't form the words fast enough, and they blew out like water from a high-pressure hose. "What are you talking about? There's nothing eating up my insides—just a bit of stomach pain."

Pyles rubbed at the back of his neck and the sweat gathered there. He sighed as if letting loose of a heavy burden. "Bronagh, we know. We've all kind of known for a while. Cancer in the belly, right? I wanted to say something before this, but you worked so hard pretending everything was fine. Us not knowing seemed to bring you comfort."

Bronagh steadied her shock as best she could. "How did you find out?"

"We noticed the way you're always touching your stomach," Conole said.

"You've lost weight, and I can't remember the last solid thing I've seen you eat," Wadim added.

Pyles flared both nostrils. "I smelled the sickness on you last spring, but I tried to tell myself it wasn't serious. I was in as bad a denial as you were, then the three of us started noticing the signs something wasn't right. It's not fair putting you on the spot like this, but after this change, my nose is back running on all cylinders. Bronagh, you're worse, a lot worse. I hate to say this, but I can smell the sickness all the way through you."

This recent revelation came as news to Wadim and Conole. They joined together to stare at Bronagh for any kind of denial. Unfortunately, the sad truth played out there in the tears and pain she no longer had to hide. Her eyes swelled with fresh misery, her mouth sagged, and she fought to speak over the sobbing.

She said, "I wasn't sure how to tell you lads without you losing hope. My son doesn't even know. How do I break the news?"

"It's all right, you don't have to pretend anymore," Conole said, leading the embrace around Bronagh, which began with him and traveled along Wadim and Pyles until it connected the four in a powerful embrace.

Pyles broke the moment when he said, "I wasn't trying to blindside you; I just couldn't stay silent any longer. I mean not with a possible solution sitting at our feet. What better place then here, what better time than this very second?"

Wadim took the blanket off the jar and stepped away like a matador twirling his cape. Conole followed along, and together he and Wadim metaphorically drew a line in the sand. Pyles picked the shovel up and used it like the arrow of a compass pointing straight down to the jar.

Bronagh could only shake her head. "What if I can't come back? What if it changes me for good?"

Conole wiped at what may have been a tear and said, "Don't worry. We'll all be waiting to make sure you're okay. You're not alone. This could be the miracle you've been praying for. That we've all been praying for."

Overhead, a plane left a white plume as it added a line of icing to the already blue frosted sky of late afternoon. Bronagh looked at it and the sun. "I don't even know if this will work during the day. I was a spirit of the night, a thing of shadows."

Pyles demonstrated a soft caress of the shovel's point. "Just make light contact and the change comes slower."

"You can control it by will if you're focused enough," Wadim added.

Bronagh contemplated the pain as the beast in her belly awoke and clawed at her insides. As if stirred by acknowledgment, the cancer pulsed like the ether but only produced pain.

Bronagh understood whatever they pondered and professed about the jar amounted to nothing but guesses. Already the jar had proved them wrong by Conole's brief transformation after he separated himself from it. If the devil worshippers wanted this jar, it couldn't be anything but bad mojo.

She had no way of knowing the outcome, but Bronagh placed her palm on the glass. She hoped for the best and looked to her friends for strength. The late winter breeze of the ether sprang forth and Bronagh forgot everything else.

An express bus labeled *fulfillment* carted all her cares away. In her return to un-life, she experienced an enlightenment few Buddhist monks would comprehend.

To the shock or her friends, Bronagh's frail body dissolved into the molecules and fundamental building blocks of the universe. The filament-like webbing of ectoplasm appeared in the air where she had once stood.

The sun's warmth pressed her toward nonexistence, but Bronagh pressed back until her incorporeal form appeared. The shadowy outline of a young girl, weeping and clutching bloody clothes—the legendary banshee of myth.

The spirit flickered above Conole, Pyles, and Wadim like the image of a failing projector. The harbinger of death manifested, and sensing the upcoming loss of life, released a long, blood-chilling wail.

The piercing shriek ruptured the silence of the afternoon. The sound tore into every open ear and punctured every normal thought. The other Fogies recoiled in a stunned silence. They understood the spirit's wail meant death for someone there. Inescapable and most likely sudden, and nothing could be done to change it.

Somewhere far off, Bronagh's consciousness seemed to exist outside of her spectral self. In a paradox of physics, she had maintained contact with the demonic jar, still able to feel the smoothness of its surface, while also having no physical form to connect her to the world.

She concentrated on breaking the connection and releasing her hold on the energy. This taxed her will as the ether flowed like a powerful drug. Bronagh pictured herself separating contact with the jar. She focused on the human warmth coming from her friends and used it as a landmark to find her way back.

The ghostly figure's wailing ended as the elderly Bronagh emerged from the cloud of collected particles used in the spirit's creation. Reality acted like a thin veil she had to step through. On the other side, her friends and the evening sun were waiting. She came to flat on her back, like a body laid out for viewing.

Pyles had a hand beneath her head, his rough callouses supporting her neck as if she had taken a tumble. "Old gal, are you okay? Say something to let us know you're okay."

"I believe I'm all right," a winded Bronagh answered.

Conole threw a blanket over the jar and said, "It might be exhaustion."

Wadim took Bronagh's car keys while Pyles escorted her to the passenger seat. Meanwhile, Conole used the spade to bury the jar beneath the pitcher's mound. He patted the earth down and hoped there wouldn't be any surprise games coming up.

Bronagh eased herself into the seat and said, "I sensed death. I even saw it for a moment before at my apartment. Here, though, I saw a terrible bleeding end. You heard my shriek, didn't you? Please tell me the truth. I must know."

Words weren't required, but Wadim nodded his head and whispered, "Yes, we heard it, but you catch your breath and try to rest. We'll check on you as soon as we're done here. We want to make sure everything's cleaned up."

"A fine idea," Bronagh said, already drifting toward sleep. "I never thought I'd say this, but later you could you sniff me? See if the sickness remains?"

Pyles took careful care closing the car door against Bronagh's feet. "Of course, once you're awake."

Wadim and Pyles crept away as Bronagh's eyes closed. Neither man said a word until well out of her earshot.

Pyles glanced back to make sure Bronagh hadn't snuck out to follow them. Seeing her still in the car, he said, "Do you think it can be avoided?"

Pyles didn't have to specify what he meant. Wadim had been brooding about the wail since hearing it.

"Most likely not, most likely one of us is already on borrowed time," Wadim said.

"But which one?" Pyles asked.

Conole, finishing up with the hole, spoke up to voice the concern each shared. "Maybe all of us," he said. "Could be none of us will survive this."

Chapter 13

Streamers of black smoke stretched up to the sky. Emergency vehicles of every kind blocked off several main roads and side streets. Most of the alleys and backways were flooded with rerouted traffic. Bronagh looked on with concern as she directed Wadim to cut across several backyards on the way to her apartment.

To their horror, Bronagh's complex couldn't be approached without penetrating a mob of bystanders and emergency service people. The blast of high-pressure water and the screech of radio chatter grew louder as they came closer to the blazing funnel that had been Bronagh's home hours before. So far luck and wind kept the smoke and heat away from the large crowd of spectators.

Before those gathered there, the retirement complex had been completely engulfed. The fire looked to be working its way from the top down. It burned hot enough that the outer concrete cracked. Heat poured off the flaming building and set the nearby trees and flowers on fire. From inside, the fire alarm blew its shrill cry. The complex had a sprinkler system, but the dry season limited the available water, making it ineffective.

Once out of the car, Bronagh scoured the shocked faces around her. She saw a few she knew, but none could provide an explanation to her questions. The other Fogies set themselves behind her and followed as she pushed into the swarm of people.

"My home," Bronagh moaned. She opened her mouth, but no noise came out as she watched everything she owned be engulfed in flames. The loss of what she witnessed momentarily ripped away her ability to process. Again, she pursed her lips but could only say, "My home…it's on fire…my home."

Wadim craned his head to look at the roof of the complex where the smoke coiled like a snake. He asked about the fire origins from a few onlookers, and the elderly man he'd seen before with similar hair said, "They said someone may have gone crazy and set the fire. Everyone inside was acting so crazy anyway. Who knows what one of them may have done?"

Wadim scoffed and said, "Perhaps an errant spark in a cluttered space caused this. It's too early to assume arson."

"None of the ambulances have their lights on. This isn't a good sign," Conole said. "Bronagh, maybe you shouldn't be here right now."

As if attempting to deal out punishment to herself, Bronagh drove a hard fist into her own thigh. She grimaced at the pain and repeated the strike a dozen more times. "You're wrong. This is exactly where I need to be. This is not a coincidence. We caused this when we brought that thing here. I caused this, thinking death is something I could cast off like an old coat. This is our doing."

Wadim grabbed her arm and said, "You don't know that."

Pyles watched firefighters move in to combat the blaze with water hoses. He sniffed and smelled ash and smoke. "You aren't the one who brought that demonic thing here—I was. This is my fault. I didn't even take a second to worry about what it could do to your home. I ruined your life tonight. I'm so sorry, Bronagh, I didn't know. I didn't mean to."

Bronagh touched Pyles's elbow and said, "I'm the one who started the Fogies because I feared facing death alone. I pulled all of you to me and set you on this path. You were only doing what you thought was right. Had I just accepted my inevitable end, none of this or us would be here, looking at the world burning. It's so hard, though, for someone who has lived for centuries to embrace the finality of dying."

Conole hitched his pants up so not to get them wet in the gathering water from the firefight. He took extra steps to avoid getting shin-deep in the growing bog of wet soot. "You didn't force us into any of this. We all have been foolish in our pursuits, but none of us lit the match that caused this. We're not arsonists."

Pyles did his best to keep Bronagh from stomping into a stream of muddy hose water, but she waved him off. Bronagh headed toward several residents being checked on by a group of paramedics. Oxygen masks covered their faces, except for Bonnie Sweeten and her gray sweater, who looked to be fit enough to shout orders at the first responders.

Oddly, rather than their normal blue and black uniforms, a great many of the police wore unmarked riot gear. This gave them the look of a single unified army. The black chest protectors, helmets, and gloves made them into a featureless death squad. The way they acted toward those gathered suggested the fire didn't happen by accident. In a world of increasing violence, the black clad police acted like enforcers for those trying to help.

Multiple volunteer firefighting groups seemed to be chipping in to help keep the dangerous fire from spreading during the drought. An entire brigade of volunteers from Eller focused their water-dousing efforts on the brown grass surrounding the building. They knew one stray spark could ignite the neighborhood.

Suddenly, the windows of the upper floors blew out and sent everyone running for cover. The heat roared into the open air, and the influx of oxygen stirred the flames like fiery tentacles. This drove the emergency responders into the street, and another blast spewed forth a fiery rain of hot cinders and ash. A great crash from inside sounded like an entire floor had given way. Black plumes of smoke rolled across the sky and smudged the horizon.

A newer resident Bronagh knew named Byron or Brian stood by an ambulance, wearing a breathing mask. He was in a robe and soot covered slacks and blood trickled out of jagged cut on his forehead. Under one arm, he clutched the painting of a house cat lounging on a sunny deck. It looked like fire had licked at the portrait's frame and charred the wood.

Brian or Byron resisted the efforts of an EMT to pull the picture away and shouted, "It's all I have left of Oliver. His ashes are gone. Leave me this. I'm not letting it go."

A shell-shocked Bronagh never moved, even as a burning sliver of glass pierced her cheek. Pyles, Wadim, and Conole stood beside her as the tiny cinders burned their skin and clothes. None of them were familiar with hell, but they recognized its terrible face in the glowing eyes of the shattered windows. Bronagh's building now resembled a burning effigy to the god of catastrophes.

A forceful hand dug into Bronagh's shoulder, and she strained to shake it loose. Sometimes she could perceive death in the air, often like a wisp of smoke, usually gone before really being noticed. Touching the jar had reawakened an old bond. Bronagh had spent her human life trying to dampen the image of the reaper, and one touch later, it was all she could see. The shadow of death lingered in the atmosphere, and she sensed its cold gaze upon her and the other Fogies.

Tears streaked her sooty face, but Bronagh made no effort to hide them. Once more someone tried to pull her away, to forcefully move her like a child who had wandered too far away Bronagh relented, to find Bonnie Sweeten facing her.

"Bonnie," Bronagh said, unable to say more as her throated threatened to close with sorrow and the acrid smoke.

Bonnie came with a lover's closeness, putting her lips almost to Bronagh's. Those same chapped lips wrinkled back over the snarling frown of a person almost driven mad under grief and strain, the same expression carried by the confused survivors of a drunk driving accident. The unbridled rage at what is seen as the ultimate cruelty of human error when the life lost is an innocent bystander. Bonnie looked at Bronagh as if she had been the drunk behind the wheel.

Bonnie's gray sweater had collected half a dozen burns. Her normally styled hair ran wild like a nest. Her eyes, red-rimmed from smoke and tears, narrowed to slits of rage.

"You and your friends had me so agitated I suffered a bad migraine. I was out of my medicine and had to run to the store. That's the only thing that kept me from being here when this place went up," Bonnie whispered.

Bronagh said, "God, Bonnie, I'm so sorry about everything. It all seems so stupid and pointless at this moment."

Bonnie wiped a tear away before it had a chance to make it to her cheek. "I should be thanking you, I guess. I was waiting for the prescription when Amy Jo from the fourth floor called me to say the most amazing thing. She said everyone here was acting peculiar, and she saw something climbing up the side of the building. She described it as a funny-looking man in a Halloween costume, like he was a corpse. A funny corpse with ropes coming out of his back." Bonnie pressed a fist into her mouth to suppress the moans threatening to turn into sobs. Her shoulders moved like pistons under the strain of holding everything back.

This description of the strange man in a Halloween costume staggered Pyles and Wadim. The two men arrived at a conclusion formed in part by each of them.

Wadim whispered to Pyles and Conole, "The zombie, the thing reanimated by the Cloves. It came here."

"For the jar," Pyles answered. "It sensed the ether, same as we did, and came here to get it back, only we were already gone."

Both men studied their surroundings more intently, as if the undead creature lurked in the shadows.

Bronagh wasn't sure what could be said. She didn't know if the right phrase or comment existed. She shielded her eyes from more hot embers and said, "Bonnie, you don't have to put yourself through this. There's nothing you could have done. Sometimes bad things just happen. You should be thankful you're alive. We all should be. Have they said if everyone made out?"

She watched the other woman tremble as the pent-up emotions wracked her body. Bonnie had become a pot of rice left covered for too long. Soon all the pressure would find a release, even if it meant a mental breakdown.

Bonnie put a palm to her brow, where the stress had begun to gather. "Don't tell me that. You of all people don't get to say anything ever again. Amy Jo, she watched this human fly go up the side of the complex. Do I have to let you guess which window it crawled into?"

Bronagh sniffled. Her legs faltered, but either Wadim or Pyles caught her. She never knew whom because they released her just as quick. "I know it's my fault. Every terrible thing that happened here tonight is because of me," she said.

Bonnie raised an accusatory finger as spittle flew from her lips. "The lucky ones who made it out say this costumed nutjob worked his way through the building, killing anyone he came across. Tell me, Bronagh, did we all suffer because you weren't home? You're a conniving foreign bitch, and you caused this. I'll pray every day that you get what's coming to you. I'll shout it from the rooftop for all to hear."

Wadim put a protective arm between the two women and almost had a chunk bitten off for his troubles. Bonnie turned feral and snapped at him and an unflinching Bronagh. Her teeth came together at the edge of Bronagh's nose.

Pyles pulled Bronagh back and said, "The crazy bitch has gone off her medication. She needs to be committed."

Bonnie might have gone for another good mouthful, but an approaching officer in swat gear caused her to depart. The rotund officer spoke into a radio and the chatter sounded like instructions to start clearing people out. A moment later, a second shorter officer joined his partner in moving the crowd back.

The taller, wider officer surveyed those gathered and said, "Excuse me, folks, we're going to need you to move to the street. We need to clear a path for the hoses."

The shorter officer waved people away from the complex's parking lot. His polished face mask reflected the image of those gathered like a mirror. He seemed to spy the Fogies and abruptly said, "Wait, were you a member of the complex's tenant committee, a Miss Bronagh O'Neil?"

Pyles decided to play lawyer and said, "I realize that crazy lady in the sweater has probably been filling your head with all kinds of nonsense. I can assure you Bronagh was with us at the time of the fire. There's no way she could have had anything to do it."

The tall and wide officer sized the Fogies up from behind his ominous helmet. "What about her accomplice? The madman who reportedly scaled the building? What about the fire starting in her apartment? I believe it might be in everyone's best interest if we moved this conversation to the police station."

"Oh, you can't believe that, can you?" Conole said, moving Bronagh away from a cloud of drifting cinders.

Wadim stomped in a puddle left by the one of the hoses, splashing everyone close to him. "This is ridiculous. You cannot go by hearsay alone."

The evening wind turned fickle and shifted to pull fresh air off the river. It stoked the flames and sent people scurrying away from the shifting heat. This breeze opened Pyles's nose and allowed him to get a good sniff of the officers. His eyes widened in comprehension.

Pyles slapped Wadim on the chest and said, "Hey, these are the same assholes that had you guys locked up. They're not the local cops, hell, they're not even troopers. They're the Deer Rose City police. These pricks don't have any authority here."

The taller officer raised his face shield and revealed Eller County's own grinning Chief Lawson, his signature belly concealed behind the body armor. "You're a sharp tack, aren't you? Maybe you folks really are psychics. Regardless, either you can come with us the easy way, or I can start cracking skulls in front of God and country. I believe you have something that is Clove property, and I would like it back."

Wadim moved so he stood shoulder to shoulder with Pyles. The pair created a natural barrier, protecting Bronagh and Conole. Wadim turned to either side to gauge the size of the remaining crowd. He said, "You're bluffing. You wouldn't be so stupid to try anything with all these witnesses around. Witnesses with cell phones and cameras just waiting to catch an authority figure doing something they shouldn't."

The chief mimicked Wadim and glanced over each shoulder and shrugged. "Your friend has a good sized knife strapped to his leg. All I have to say is he went for it. Maybe I can't justify roughing up an entire group of AARP members, but my career can take the heat of knocking one of you stupid."

Wadim took his turn to slap Pyles on the chest. Wadim looked to Conole and Bronagh and said, "This is no coincidence these monsters being here. They set the fire, not the thing they summoned. This zombie might have caused a lot of carnage, but it didn't set this blaze. It doesn't like fire, and they know this."

This time the smaller police officer spoke up. He took a threatening step forward, but stopped short of physically touching any of them. "What if we did? You can't prove anything anyhow. Trust me, we did you all a favor. It was a slaughterhouse in there. Less evidence for everyone this way. Besides, it didn't come here because it wants to retire. It came here looking for something, and we have a pretty good idea what it is."

Conole mimicked the stranger from the store and took hold of his cane like a bat. "You set this fire and killed how many people because you didn't want your little secret getting out? If karma exists at all, that thing is roasting inside this very moment, and you'll end up joining it."

"Fat chance of either happening," the smaller officer said.

Chief Lawson put his face shield back down. He raised his baton and leveled it at Wadim. "I knew you and your friends were up to something. I took you for routine snoops with nothing better to do than chase legends about cults. But I did some sleuthing of my own, and when Miss O'Neil's address came across our bandwidth, I put two and two together. Now that I know our other friend came here, I imagine you are more than just regular snoops.”

“Did someone have to help you with the equation of two and two?” Wadim said, setting his feet wide and his toes pointed out, like a man readying for a nasty scrap.

Chief Lawson moved the baton so each of The Fogies had a turn to be staring down the wrong end of it. “I get it. You’re betting on the threat of consequences stopping me. You need to know consequences are something I’d have to worry about afterward. I have several commendations, medals, and a record so clean you could eat off it. I could beat one of you to death while the whole town burns and not have to answer for it until the investigations concludes in about six months.”

“I think you’re bluffing,” Conole replied. “We all have clean records as well and maybe we left a post about devil-worshipping police on our website.”

The chief shrugged. “I hope you did. That will only make it easier to say how crazy and delusional you acted. You think things like this can’t happen, but they happen every day. So long as the pizzas keep getting delivered and the Internet doesn’t slow down, no one cares. If I go under investigation, I have six months to target every person you care about—children, grandchildren, friends of friends. You go ahead and ask yourselves if I seem like the forgive and forget type.”

The smaller officer said, “Shit, I say we could pin the fire on them. Goddamn delusional old pricks, seeing Satanists under every rock and behind every curtain. The lot went crazy and set fire to the building to save the town."

Bronagh took the chance to speak up. "I believe the things you say. No one else should have to suffer. We're no threat to you, and I want to prove that. What can we do to facilitate your mercy?"

Wadim turned his head quickly enough that his dyed sweat sprayed across Pyles's shoulder. "Have you taken absence of your wits? These animals set this fire and sealed the fate of your neighbors and everything you owned. They know about as much about mercy as a wild dog does."

Bronagh lowered her chin, allowing the river of tears to run wild through the smears of soot. "Our vanity brought that thing here in the first place. We're just as much to blame. I don't want to see another person get hurt because we refuse to accept our fate."

Chief Lawson lowered the baton and said, "You come quietly back to the station with us. You answer all our questions, and there's no reason this can't end peacefully."

Pyles pursed his lips and made a raspberry sound. "You mean get us away from all these witnesses so you can waterboard us. Cut us into a bunch of little pieces for an easy cleanup. Nuts to that. You're not taking me without a fight."

Wadim drew back his arm as if to swing for the fences. "The finest idea I've ever heard."

"No," Bronagh said, holding both Pyles and Wadim back. "There's been so much death here today, I can't take anymore. We'll go and do as they say. I'm sure some agreement can be reached."

The chief gestured toward the street, where several squad cars were parked. "In a single file, I want you to casually walk to those police cruisers and put your cell phones on the hood. We'll be right behind you, so don't try anything cute. If you need more convincing, look at every emergency person here. More than half of them are with us. If you think that's a bluff, you better be ready to bet the farm on it."

Conole tossed his cane aside and said, "What of the zombie? Where did it go?"

Lawson's chuckles seeped out of the helmet. The thick plastic added a hollowness to the already off-putting cackle. "Don't worry. I have a feeling it will turn up sooner or later. One problem at a time, though. Now again, it would be smart to check the numbers, as they favor our side."

Bronagh took her cell phone out of her pocket and dropped it at the feet of the policemen. "Lads, it's not my place to tell you what to do, but I'm through being selfish. You do whatever it is you think is best. I won't hold it against you."

Pyles snorted. "I'm not going anywhere with them. I figure they sent that wall- crawling thing here to do their dirty work."

Chief Lawson interrupted with a harsh laugh that came across as maybe the first real emotion he'd showed in many moons. "It hardly matters where the truth lies because this is a certainty. The golem is now awake and hungry."

"Because you fools woke it up," Wadim said, his accusation cutting the chief off.

Lawson's leather gloves creaked as he tightened his grip on the baton. "You have it in your head you know something about this golem. Let me clue you in: You don't know diddly-squat. You see, it might have survived this blaze. We won't really know for sure until the coroner gets a chance to comb through everything. Assuming it did, once the thing finds the fetus again, it's not going to be good for any of us. It can sense the demonic baby, and by it showing up, I'm guessing the glass jar was here."

Pyles shrugged. "You can quit trying to scare us. Your bogeyman had the jar once and buried it like a dog. Big deal, says I."

The police officers straightened at this. The smaller of the officers said, "Not just regular sleuths, huh? But still, you don't get it. You see, the reanimated corpse must nap every so often to let itself recharge. However, the more blood it gets the less it requires sleep. In the wake of a feast like this, it's not going to have to sleep for days."

Chief Lawson snorted. "At the beginning, it was more machine than monster, but amped up on the blood, suddenly it's a lot more monster. Machines don't have wills or purpose. Monsters, on the other hand, have a lot of both."

Conole said, "Is there any way we can stop it?"

"We've said all we're going to say," the chief replied. "Single file, let's go and not a peep or cross look or even so much as a sideways fart until we're on the road. We won't put you in cuffs because that might arouse suspicions. Don't take this as me being a kind soul."

With her head hung low, eyes downcast, Bronagh went to the first of the police cruisers. Her surrender drained the remaining Fogies of their resolve, and the others followed her lead. The chief and his men fell in to flank them from the rear.

The smaller of the policemen jogged ahead to open the back door to each of the cruisers. Outside the cars were unmarked and nondescript, but inside the vehicles had prisoner cages, radios, and attachable magnetic lights for the roofs.

Chief Lawson collected the other cell phones and put Pyles in one car and Wadim in next. Conole and Bronagh had to share the back seat of the chief's cruiser. In a final act of defiance, Pyles tossed his knife into the ditch across from the road rather than let them take it.

Surprisingly, no one paid the police and their passengers any attention. Once the traffic along the street cleared, the cruisers departed in succession. Conole and Bronagh sat in silence during the ride, holding hands for comfort. In his own car, Pyles sang as loud and off-key as possible, while in Wadim's case, the trip started with a single question.

Chapter 14

Wadim didn't need the ether or Bronagh's warning to recognize a bad situation when he saw one. The Fogies being carted off like enemies of the state seemed about as bad as it could get. He suspected unless someone did something none of them would be leaving the police barracks alive. His intuition, or what Pyles would have called "the gut" had he been there, told Wadim the Fogies had become a loose end and warranted cleaning up.

He wasn't sure what could be done, especially factoring in the superior numbers and firepower they faced. Wadim had the outline of an idea, but it all dependent on the officer escorting him wanting to prove himself. Even then the steps would have to play out just so.

"Tell me, do you want me to take you to the jar?" Wadim asked once he and the smaller deputy were alone.

He leaned forward until his mouth almost touched the prisoner's cage separating the back and front seats. "It's a bit out of the way, but I get the feeling you're a man willing to make a deal. I mean, after all don't you Cloves barter with demons? I can promise my fee will not be as high."

The smaller officer gave the cage a good smack with his palm. "Let me guess, you don't want us to hurt you or your friends. Why should I listen to anything you have to say? Chief Lawson is going to get the location out of you regardless."

Wadim opened his hands as if to say they held no surprises. "Do not be misconstrued; those aren't my friends. They are chains around my neck. Those simpletons thought it ideal to put the jar in the ground, willfully ignoring what it could do."

The smaller officer tried to steel himself as if he wasn't intrigued. Although he didn't react with the same violence this time as Wadim drew closer to the cage. Like all immature pups, full of piss and vinegar, the deputy wanted to cut his teeth and prove his worth. The older, more experienced Wadim knew this because he had donned the same dunce cap of youth once himself. In fact, he had been counting on this.

Wadim tried to keep the desperateness from his voice. "I can lead you to the jar. It's not far, and the credit can be all yours. Think of the stress it will save your chief. He may promote you."

The deputy shifted to stare at his prisoner. The probing glare of a police training going against the harsh glare of bloody nights under black, starless skies. "And what do *you* get out of this?"

Wadim deliberately waited before replying. He allowed a quarter mile of road to pass, as if he had maybe reconsidered the offer. Finally, he said, "Let's not be coy. I want to be a Clove; I want to be one of you. You have vast resources and knowledge, and I want to share in this. I believe our goals align—power, influence. These are things that I crave as well."

The deputy's lack of a response motivated Wadim to break the cardinal rule of the Fogies. "I have experience with the supernatural that could be of use. You see, I used to be a Nosferatu, the walking dead, a vampire. This is how our little group formed itself. The tall hillbilly was a werewolf, the old lady what you would call a banshee, and the short stack came from the wee folk. I ask you to put aside your disbelief and consider the truth of such a thing. Consider what this could do for your coven. I can assure you it is merely the tip of the iceberg."

The deputy picked up the microphone for his car radio and pressed the talk button. He cleared his throat and said, "Chief, this guy is saying some weird stuff."

The chief's voice carved a harsh beat through the static filled line. "Be advised I thought I said I wanted radio silence while we're in route to the station, complete silence. Do we have a good copy, or should I spell it out?"

Wadim's escort noticeably paused before responding. He held the microphone, but hesitated pressing the talk button. His jaw tensed as one not accustomed or appreciative of being chastised.

"We got a good copy here," he said. The officer slowly placed the microphone back on its hook. He put a ragged thumbnail to his mouth and chewed on the meager amount of cuticle left. The rest of his fingers looked like they had also been gnawed on.

Wadim could see the next part would be where the final pitch had to be made. He thought the chief had either intentionally or unintentionally bristled the short hairs of Wadim's escort.

Concentrating on the right tone of condolence, Wadim said, "There you have it: He's all but absolved you of any punishment for taking a detour. You were going to tell him, but he cut you off. Think of the crow your chief will be served when in walks the fetus and a potential new member."

Never taking his eyes off the road, the shorter officer said, "How far are we talking?"

The front seat's headrest hid Wadim's grin. "Are you acquainted with the Tee- ball field?"

The officer nodded, "The memorial field? Yeah, I use to play in the Christian youth league when I was a kid."

"Splendid and ironic," Wadim said as he slipped into the shadows growing in the rear of the vehicle. "Your jar is buried under the pitcher's mound. I even know where we can get a shovel to dig it up."

The officer turned to stare at Wadim. Once more, he looked to be using his gaze to try to intimidate the older man. "For your sake, I'm hoping this isn't a case of dementia leading me on a wild goose chase. I shouldn't have to tell you how bad it will be if we get to the ball field and there's nothing there."

"I'm too old to try to escape. What benefit is there for lying?" Wadim said.

"I don't know, but you just remember I'm not above shooting you."

Wadim tipped his head. "I do not doubt this."

Both Wadim and the deputy were preoccupied with ideas of how the night might go. As such, neither caught sight of the thin, silver-threaded hose slither across the road behind them. Pyles could have taken a single whiff and been able to tell them what danger lurked in the woods. Bronagh might have seen the shadow of death hanging over the cruiser and foretold what was to come. Conole could have warned of dark energy following them.

These things however were of little importance as the unmarked car sped off toward the ball field. Even if Wadim had known, it would have made little difference. In his heart, he suspected the time of the Old Fogies was coming to an end.

Chapter 15

Wadim thought the baseball field took on a different almost malevolent appearance in the dark—so far from civilization, and yet so well maintained it looked like some secret place where spirits gathered. The symmetry of the field and deserted bleachers suggested a sacred site. Like the Aztec temples of old in which sacrifices were offered to forgotten gods while devout followers watched. Maybe it was touching the jar earlier or maybe nerves, but he sensed something foreboding about the area.

He didn't need a psychiatrist to tell him the reason his mind made such a connection. Wadim continued to dig under armed supervision, hoping the others were still breathing and hadn't been sacrificed.

"I didn't bring you out here to look at the stars. You're supposed to be digging, unless there's nothing to dig up," the shorter officer said, while aiming his gun at Wadim.

From the edge of the parking lot, the officer kept surveillance, pistol ready. He had attached a pen light to the weapon and used the bright illumination to keep watch of his prisoner while leaning on the chain link fence.

"I'm sorry. I move slowly because of caution. I imagine you don't want the glass accidently shattered. I recall the velvet liner of the trunk at the antique shop, the thickness of the interior. I assume harnessing the power within involves keeping this dead baby contained inside the jar," Wadim said.

The shorter officer groaned, "If you're that worried about it, use your hands. I'm losing my patience, and this could be bad for you."

"If I get down, I may have trouble returning to my feet," Wadim said.

The officer made the sign of the devil's horns with his pinky and pointer finger, popularized by heavy metal music. He spat through the space between them and said, "By the black goat may a hundred babies be birthed stillborn so I might never grow old. With the blessing of brimstone may never, never come."

Wadim pretended he didn't hear or see the sacrilegious prayer. While not exactly a fan of any religion, he could say the Christian god at least preached love, but what did the black goat believe in? What were the Satanic Cloves willing to do to appease it? He didn't want to linger on the answer.

Wadim scraped away a clod of dirt and the blanketed lid of the jar peeked out from the bottom of the hole. Upon seeing this discovery, the officer carefully moved forward a few feet.

The officer leveled the gun at Wadim's back, and neither man spoke for a moment. Wadim dug more and exposed the glass and its demonic contents.

Finally, with the jar was fully revealed, the officer said, "You go ahead and use one hand and toss that shovel over by the shed. You're going to bring the fetus out of the hole then crawl away from it. No crazy movements, no trying anything stupid."

Wadim wiped the dirt from his hands and put pressure to a back aching from all the effort. He tossed the shovel aside and eased into the hole. "I'll do as instructed. I pride myself on avoiding stupid or foolish decisions. But permit me one question: Have you or the others interacted with this jar before?"

While Wadim struggled to be as careful as possible, the shorter officer answered, "No, this thing was Jonas's responsibility. He dealt with it and the golem. These were his big ideas."

"Interesting," Wadim said with a hidden smile.

The blanket and jar came up quickly despite the delicate way Wadim handled them. The shorter officer anxiously tapped his boot. His excitement caused him to act like an overstimulated pet in need of a walk.

"You keep your head facing the hole. Now I want you do your best Fido-the-good-dog impersonation. You crawl over there toward first base, away from the glass."

"Okay, just mind the trigger. We're all friends here," Wadim whispered.

Wadim slipped a dirt-covered hand up to the glass. The energy immediately flooded into him. The tingling surged along his flesh as though he had stuck his finger in the world's largest light socket. The jar reacted to his touch and sent waves of mystical energy in every direction, like a powerful aura illuminating the empty and stagnant night.

"You can go ahead and quit touching it," the deputy mumbled, sounding less sure of himself than before. Wadim saw this nonreaction to the energy as a perfect example of how the jar's effects weren't universal.

A grinning Wadim clutched the jar under his arm, careful to keep skin touching the glass. When he rose to his feet and faced the deputy, Wadim's eyes were a bottomless, bloodshot red. The real fangs that Wadim had yearned to have once more slowly emerged like the thermometers for a cooked turkey.

The Satanic officer raised his gun and discovered the flashlight's beam unable to pierce the gloom. He tried for his radio, but nothing came through the line but a hissing static.

With growing alarm creeping into his voice, the officer said, "You better stop right where you are. I want you to put the fetus on the ground and put your hands above your head."

The darkness of the night recognized the draconic hunger in Wadim and sought to sate it. The wind, seemingly becoming a nocturnal beast under his control, carried Wadim across the infield, cloaking him in a formless shadow.

"The Devil protect me," the shorter officer said.

"The greatest trick the devil ever played was convincing fools to worship him," Wadim whispered as he drew close.

The officer shot at the clawed hands moving toward him. The bullets found their target, but did nothing to halt Wadim's progress. Unharmed and unfazed by the gun, Wadim seized the officer's exposed throat and pulled him in to meet a mouth full of razor-sharp teeth.

"The dance stops for all of us sooner or later," Wadim whispered just before he bit into the soft warm flesh of his first kill in almost 50 years. "Unfortunately, this is your sooner."

The vampire Wadim buried his fangs into the man's neck and warm blood sprayed across his face. Frantically, the dying officer fired his pistol until the gun clicked empty. With the last of his strength, he tried the radio, but unconsciousness claimed him first.

Wadim fed until the man's heart ceased pumping. To be sure, he checked for a pulse and found none. Satisfied the officer had shuffled off the mortal coil, he turned out the dead man's pockets for the cruiser's keys. With the jar still under one arm, Wadim deposited the body into the trunk.

His plan had worked, but the next part would be the real test. By taking this life, Wadim had crossed a line from which there might be no return. He believed in his heart of hearts that his friends were in danger. He also believed the next part would not be as easy. It would require him to travel into the belly of the beast.

"I have you though, don't I?" Wadim said to the demonic child within the jar. Still unmoving, the preserved body gave no indication one way or another.

Wadim turned the cruiser around and hoped there wouldn't be any sort of police roll call until his business in Deer Rose had been concluded. All the supernatural power in the world couldn't affect this. Wadim would have to hope the universe favored them over the Cloves.

Reluctantly, he strapped the jar into the passenger seat of the cruiser. With a great deal of effort, Wadim severed the connection and returned to being a mortal. It pained him to do so, but he needed to be clear-headed enough to drive. The car was unmarked, and it was dark, which he prayed would aid him in going unnoticed behind the wheel.

The cruiser steered easy enough and getting it back onto the interstate proved unchallenging. Wadim tried to keep under the speed limit, but his foot kept creeping toward the gas pedal. Already Wadim worried he might be too late. Just outside the Deer Rose limits, he pulled over and retrieved the deputy's gun from the trunk. He hoped it wouldn't come down to a shootout.

Chapter 16

Once arriving at their destination, Bronagh and Conole were rushed to an unfamiliar part of the courthouse. They were shoved through a metal door hidden at the bottom of the outside stairwell. They didn't see Pyles or Wadim anywhere and wondered about their safety.

Chief Lawson and a female officer did the escorting. The female officer's nameplate said "Cook," and her face remained passive during the process. She kept a crackling stun gun on the Fogies as they were led in a windowless subbasement of the courthouse.

The dank halls were comprised of a rough and heavy stone like a medieval dungeon. Rows of dangling glass bulbs protected by small cages cast an eerie white light over what could have been a cold war bomb shelter.

Bronagh didn't see any other way out besides the heavy-looking iron door behind them. There were no windows or sounds other than the echoes of their own footfalls. The wide, ominous halls allowed Lawson and his crony to march Bronagh and Conole double file into a large square stone room fitted with leg shackles on the floor.

The rusty leg chains were attached above a spot on the floor carrying the design of a large red pentagram etched into the floor. The bloodlike stains running from the shackles to a small grate in the pentagram's center suggested the space might have served a darker purpose.

Chief Lawson aimed his pistol at them and used the barrel to gesture toward the shackles. "In case you're wondering, the walls are soundproof. Any shot might echo like crazy, but they wouldn't so much as hear a low *ping* outside. So you do what I say, and no one gets hurt."

Conole wanted no part of this room. Demonic magic stained everything both in the physical and spiritual sense. The residual taint of the foul rituals affected him like an allergy of the spirit. He felt his soul wanting to surrender to the helplessness this place fostered. Terrible suffering had happened here for the favor of ancient evils.

Maybe sensing this distress, Bronagh tried to rebuff the encroaching fear the only way she knew how. She gathered herself up and said, "Why did you bring us to this dungeon? I thought we would talk and be let go. Can't we do that upstairs in the station, like decent human beings? We came here on good faith."

Chief Lawson filled the doorway leading to the room with his large frame and kept the gun on Bronagh. He knew this would neuter any courage Conole might have mustered. Not that the shorter man could have offered much of a resistance.

"I should shoot you for that. What, if anything, about me suggests decency and good faith?"

"That badge should make you decent," Bronagh said.

Chief Lawson answered with a scowl. "Nowadays these things are handed out like candy at Halloween. The Cloves got me this position. They helped me to be where I am. If you think this badge means decency, you haven't been watching the news."

Officer Cook moved over by the shackles. "No more stalling. You're going in restraints. I will not tell you a second time. This means you, half-man, come on, let's go."

The chief's female goon prodded Conole along with her stun gun. When he resisted, she clicked the button as a warning. The two hooked prongs of the device immediately crackled with thousands of volts of electricity. The smell of hot metal filled the air.

Conole moaned as the electricity arced dangerously close to him. "Just a little patience is all I ask. I can get there, but it takes me a minute."

Bronagh started forward, but the chief's pistol stopped her. The sense of death returned, and she imagined its shadow being within touching distance now.

She tried logic and said, "He has leg and knee problems— all the shoving isn't necessary. If you allow him a moment, he'll get there. Here, start with me. I'll show you we're not resisting."

Bronagh took nervous half steps until her feet rested on an old blood stain next to one of the metal cuffs. She turned her attention to the walls and ceiling, where dozens of painted symbols marked this room as one large altar to the demonic. As she studied the hellish art, the female deputy secured Conole with one of the chains around his ankle.

Conole jumped when Officer Cook jabbed him with the stun gun. She laughed at his response and showed she hadn't pressed the trigger button.

Conole swallowed hard and said, "You're truly demented."

Like a sick joke, Bronagh noticed the symbol of the ether amongst the different images on the wall, but something about it looked off. In an act of perversion rather than the traditional raindrop appearance the symbol had been inverted to look like a net cast about the planet. Many of the Satanic practices she'd observed seemed to elevate inversion or perversion of the sacred.

The chief followed her gaze and opened his arms as if to embrace the painted head of a three-horned goat with a snakelike tongue gazing down from above the doorway.

The Chief said, "As a good man once said, 'The path to paradise begins in hell,' now isn't that the truth?"

Bronagh focused on Conole and replied, "That's not how the phrase goes, but I can tell you there is no greater sorrow than to recall our times of joy in wretchedness."

Chief's Lawson's focus remained on the goat as if nothing else existed. "Do me a favor, Officer Cook, and make sure their restraints are nice and tight."

Lawson went into the hall and left Cook to watch them. His absence lasted only few minutes. Pyles's angry shouts suddenly broke the silence as his shrieking reverberated off the stone halls. The chief and another officer appeared and forced the bruised mountain man into the room.

Pyles stumbled toward the shackles and fell hard on his shoulder. He groaned, cussed, and looked to be favoring a swollen hand. He stared a cold, calculating death at the officer escorting him.

This new officer had brown hair the same color of wood varnish. He still wore the generic black riot gear from the fire, but had taken off the helmet to fix his hair. He licked cracked lips and giggled like a psychopath at seeing the state of Pyles's friends.

Pyles took a quick inventory of the others and of their surroundings. "It always smells like ass in this police station. I don't think any of you know how to wipe. I can teach a class if you need it. Day one, how to keep it from getting under your fingernails."

Officer Cook clipped the stun gun to her belt. She double-checked Bronagh's chains and announced them secure. She whistled for Pyles like a dog and pointed at the next set of empty shackles. This would line the Fogies up like the paper dolls and put them directly over the bloodstained drain.

"Go ahead over there, because you wouldn't want the lady here to have to repeat herself, would you?" Chief Lawson said. He used the pistol to draw a line between Bronagh and Conole, demonstrating the order in which he would shoot should Pyles resist.

At seeing this, Pyles surrendered what sparse fight remained and joined his friends. His ankles were too big for the shackle and the metal bit into his flesh, but the female officer couldn't even pretend to be concerned.

Pyles lifted his pants leg for them and said, "Things like this come back you, believe that."

Conole swayed on his feet, the bad atmosphere influencing him toward malaise. He tested the limit of the chains and found the metal kept him from going anywhere.

Conole ended up the closest to the drain and tried to avoid stepping on any of the old blood. "We have done nothing to deserve this."

Chief Lawson spun the signet ring on his wedding finger around and held it under one of the bulbs. He marveled at the way it shined beneath the iridescent light. Something about it seemed to transfix him. He marveled at it and said, "You came here because you were concerned, and you had every right to be. You have been fooling around in Clove affairs, and I aim to see that stops tonight. As soon as the fourth member of this quartet arrives, we can begin. Roy, go radio Stellmire. See where he is. I want to make sure he didn't run into any snags."

The officer who brought Pyles in, Stellmire, the one with the demented laugh, did an about-face. He frowned at the possibility of missing out on the questioning, but did as he was told.

"All this is unnecessary," Bronagh said. "We'll tell you whatever you want. There's no reason for anyone to get hurt."

Chief Lawson slipped a pocketknife out of his pants pocket. With great, almost tender-like care, he opened the blade so the Fogies could see the literal and figurative point. Lawson showed the knife the same dark respect he displayed for the ring. Something about being here allowed him to reveal the odder parts of his personality.

The chief swayed as if he heard music and danced with the knife. "This is where the hurting begins. This is where pain and salvation meet. You can minimize the pain by telling me the truth. Where is the fetus, and how did you find it in the first place?"

Pyles put his injured hand into his healthy one. "I'm the guy you should be talking to. I'm the bloodhound who sniffed it out. That zombie of yours has a unique scent. Unique enough that it led me right to your buddy, the preserved abortion."

"Bullshit," Officer Cook said. She started forward, but Chief Lawson stopped her. He put the knife to her shoulder and smiled.

"Make me believe you," Lawson said.

Pyles took a whiff of the air and poked his tongue between his teeth to get the taste of it. "I can tell you like avocado on your egg sandwiches and generic grape soda. I can also tell you use lemon dish soap and laundry detergent with a hint of pine."

Lawson sniffed at his uniform. He took a big whiff of the air and with a shrug said, "That's a pretty good trick. I had an avocado egg salad sandwich for lunch and a grape soda at the fire. Go ahead and tell me all about sniffing out the fetus and about the golem. Keep on convincing me you have more to say."

Conole rubbed his thigh where the muscles were cramping into painful knots. "You're scared of it, aren't you? The golem, or zombie, or whatever it is. It has you quaking in your knickers. That's why you're acting so off-kilter, isn't it?"

"Fear is the smart reaction," Officer Cook said. "Just hope we can get to the fetus before it does."

Pyles gave a dry laugh. "We chucked that glass jug of yours into the deepest, swampiest marsh around. The thing really gave us the heebie-jeebies and caused the folks in her building to act a little bonkers. You'll need scuba gear, but I reckon you can find it."

Chief Lawson ran the knife blade along the doorframe, scraping away a bit of dust gathered in the cracks. "I hope for your sake you're lying. There isn't a marsh deep enough to stop the golem. Allow me to spell this out for you. If it gets hold of the fetus, we're all in trouble. You see, the fetus will call to it until it answers, no matter the distance. If we can get the jar back, there's still a chance we can control this monster. We can stop it from going berserk, from carrying out whatever dark desire is now driving it."

Bronagh discovered the boost of adrenaline from the jar and the fire had fled her. An extreme fatigue stepped in to take its place. She tried to rally herself and said, "This is your fault. You and your followers are the fools who brought that thing back to life. If it's so dangerous, why have it here in the first place? You knew who built it. What good could possibly come from a Nazi death machine?"

Chief Lawson put the knife away and returned to the pistol. Like a kid losing interest, he swapped to a different toy. He danced the barrel of the gun between the prisoners, letting it linger on each of the geezers until they flinched.

Chief Lawson settled the gun on Bronagh and said, "You can thank Jonas, the owner of the antique store, for that. He's the one who arranged for the golem's remains to be shipped overseas along with the jar. Poor delusional Jonas had it in his head he could use the golem as an enforcer. I for one never believed he would succeed where the Germans failed. I must admit that makes me a bit of dreamer."

Pyles strained in the metal shackles. He didn't like Lawson waving the gun around. It was the careless act of a psychopath. "The biggest mistake you and your followers made, besides your religious choices, was assuming the golem could be controlled by anything mortal. Also, I hate to be the one to tell you this, but that demon spawn isn't as dead as you think."

At mention of the demon spawn, Officer Cook drew their attention to the small drawing of a winged demon flying towards a painted moon. The likeness to the thing in the jar was unmistakable. Officer Cook said, "Even the damned have their prophecies and saints."

Pyles studied the painting and said, "That fetus called to us. It wants to be set free, and I don't think it cares who does it. Us, the zombie, or you guys."

Rubbing his chin, Lawson said, "What you say makes sense. Jonas told me something similar. He said he hallucinated and watched the grave-robbing scene of some old horror movie. I thought he was crazy, but he swore the fetus was telling him to try to animate the golem. Maybe our little specimen has been orchestrating all this death and carnage?"

"Nonsense," Bronagh replied. "If anyone is responsible, it's you and not some 50-year-old corpse or a demon's stillbirth."

Officer Cook spat at Bronagh, just missing her face. "You're awfully judgmental when your own colleague admits to being summoned by it. You don't know what you're doing, but we have ancient text and manuscripts. We can properly use the jar to stop the golem before it grows any stronger."

Chief Lawson had gone back to his game of the dancing gun barrel. He moved it from Fogie to Fogie, delighting at the unease it caused. "I'm growing tired of this. We can do what you could not, because we understand what sacrifice means. Maybe it's about time you did as well."

What happened next did so in a terrible nightmare-like slow motion that magnified the horrors for those forced to watch. Chief Lawson raised the gun and pulled the trigger with a thunderous echo. The shot crashed in the small room and the sound of it echoed long after Conole's lifeless body crumpled onto the stone floor. His head snapped back as part of his scalp and skull vanished.

"Oh god, no," Pyles moaned, trying to interject himself in the path of the bullet, but the shackles kept him in place. "Don't look, Bronagh, turn away. You don't need to see this."

Bronagh shrieked and fell to her knees in tears. She stretched the shackle until the tendons in her ankle popped, and she put the tips of her fingers on Conole's shoe. "No, oh Conole, no, no, no. Please no. I did this. I caused this…no, no, please no."

Bronagh knew her friend was gone. She knew it like she knew they were all going to follow him if the chief had his way. She had felt the grim shadow of death, and now it had arrived to claim the sweetest amongst them.

Conole, who had called on every wedding anniversary after her husband had died to see how she was doing; Conole, a man denied his childhood by being forced into adulthood when his connection to the ether was severed. Yet he always carried a piece of that vulnerable innocence, as if blessed to be eternally young.

"Conole, bud, say something, Conole, tell me you're okay." Pyles redoubled his efforts and yanked on the chain, but the metal held him as sure as gravity. Blood trickled from the cuff as the iron dug into the skin of his ankle.

Pyles had a fair amount of knowledge about guns. Enough to know the damage at that range would have been fatal. The statistics ran the same every time the scene replayed in his head. Conole was gone. Pyles could cover his eyes and look away, but the smell of hot gunpowder and brain matter infiltrated his nose.

"If you're smart, you'll shoot me next, because I swear to God or the devil or whoever…I'm going to grind my boots into your throat," Pyles growled.

Lawson bowed before the painting of the goat head and said, "I, your humble servant, offer this weak soul as flesh upon the altar of the profane. To all things that slither on their belly."

Officer Cook studied the remains of Conole and swooned as if in rapture like the ether. "You know, I reckon we can consider the lines of communication truly open at this point."

"Agreed. It's time the truth comes out. No more lies from any of us," Lawson hissed.

The chief's mouth snapped open at an impossible angle. His jaws cracked, revealing a hideously long, forked tongue inside a terrible inhuman maw.

The chief and Officer Cook's skin both began to shift and change, undergoing a hellish metamorphosis. Their flesh took on a dull green shade like scales. As a horrified Bronagh and Pyles watched, the pentagram beneath them blackened. When the chief and his deputy looked up to laugh, they had the slitted yellow eyes of a reptile.

Chapter 17

The room became a floodgate of foul odors and terrible hellish sounds, the magnitude of which Pyles had never encountered before. The stench of rot and fire became too much…way too much. He screamed as the pain threatened to tear his sinuses in half. The sensory section of his brain sought the darkness of fainting in a final attempt to stave off the fatal overload.

Pyles collapsed, and Bronagh called his name, but the big man offered no response. The serpentine-looking Officer Cook and Chief Lawson stood at the edge of the black pentagram. They chanted in a whispering unison and seemed to lose themselves in the reveal of their true demonic enslaved selves.

"You animals, you monsters…you didn't have to do this. Oh, God, Conole, I'm so sorry. This is my fault. You didn't have to hurt anyone; we would have given the jar back to you," Bronagh said.

Her comment was ignored as the demonic whispering became a solemn silence like a moment of remembrance. At its conclusion, Lawson's jaw opened with the wideness of a carry-on bag to show an inner mouth rotted like a festering wound.

Officer Cook's hideously elongated tongue found the Chief's and the two intertwined like bodies wrapped in the act of love. The moment only ended when Lawson, lost in pleasure, raised the gun and fired into the ceiling.

Cook whipped her tongue around and brought the stun gun up. She intended to shock herself. She stopped short of making contact, and let her tongue lick the electrified prongs.

She turned her yellow eyes to Bronagh and hissed, "Okay, old woman, tell us what you were really planning with the fetus, or your death won't be as quick as your friend's."

A groggy Pyles came to as blood poured from his overworked nose. "You leave her alone. Come on…ask me about your ugly-ass pet baby. Get a little closer, and I'll stick that stun toy up your ass. I'll show you a real good time. I'll skin you and make me a pair of snakeskin cowboy boots, good, honky-tonking boots. You want to go honkey-tonkin'?"

"We hid it under the pitcher's mound of the little league field," Bronagh said as her chest hitched with a quiet sobbing. "I swear on my life. You can look for yourself and see."

Cook walked the border of the pentagram, going heel to toe. She traveled like the minute hand of a clock, working her way around the circle. She squatted over Conole's dead body and savored the carnage before her with a small clap, as if requesting an encore. "We most certainly will, and I kind of hope it's not there," she said.

Chief Lawson holstered his weapon and said, "However mad you are, or whatever mental, spiritual, physical fortitude you figure you might have, you'd be smart to remember we're the police. We can pick your grandkids up right from the school, and nobody would even ask us why."

"You don't have to threaten us," Pyles shouted. "She's telling you exactly where the jar is. What the else do you want?"

"Answers," Officer Cook said.

"That's the size of it," Lawson replied. "You see, there's a big question that's been bugging me since we picked you up at the fire. The fetus caused all those other folks to act like grade schoolers, and yet you seemed fine. So I start running down possible explanations, but I keep coming up shorthanded in the answer departments. I enjoy a good mystery, heck, probably every cop does, but this thing here has me stumped."

As painful as it was to do, Bronagh stood up and pointed at their depiction of the ether. "We were affected in a different way. The thing in the jar called us because we weren't always human. I see you have the ether on the wall, so you know what it is. The four of us we all had a connection to it in our previous lives. We're still sensitive to it. You could say we're in recovery from being the things out there in the dark."

Pyles nodded. "I was infected with lycanthrope in my twenties, and that's how I can smell everything on you."

The still snakelike Chief Lawson breathed the rotting air in deep. He moved as if to swim through the pentagram's black smoke. "I've not heard anything so crazy in some time. You're saying you're a werewolf, and this jar—our jar—called to you because of this? Color me curious, but maybe we should cut you open and see if your insides are different?"

Officer Roy, the policeman who had brought Pyles in, reappeared at the doorway. His expression said something had happened. He held his radio up and said, "Central to Stellmire, Stellmire are you 10-17 to the station, please respond. Chief, I can't get Stellmire on the radio, and he should have been back by now."

Pyles and Bronagh shared a startled look when their skins prickled over in a rising tide of the ether. The Cloves turned their heads to the hall, showing they felt it as well. The energy meant one thing. Someone had brought the jar there.

Chief Lawson addressed his deputies while he stared at the pentagram. "Go post at the door, and keep your eyes peeled. Don't draw your weapons, but leave the holsters unsnapped. I don't want anyone to overact and jump at shadows, but if you see the golem, fall back and open fire."

Officer Roy's Adam's apple climbed up his throat as he swallowed sharply. He didn't seem bothered by the chief's or Cook's reptile appearance. "Shit, you don't really think it would come here, do you? I mean…why, for what purpose?"

Cook's skin lost its scaly-looking rash over a few quick seconds, possibly driven away by fear. In an unbelievably short time, she looked all too human once again. "Chief, we're not going to let this thing come in here, are we? If Roy is right, we're going to need bigger guns, way bigger."

The chief put a finger to his lips, indicating he had heard enough from everyone. "What we did tonight might have drawn it to us. If it is here, we'll give these two up for an offering. It still might not be too late for us to make use of that thing and bring it over to our side."

The deputies departed, but the lack of speed on Officer Cook's part suggested she didn't appreciate being put in this position. Despite what he told them, the chief moved his gun from the holster to the waistband of his belt for a quicker draw.

Pyles went as far as the shackles would reach and spat at the chief's feet. "For what you did to Conole, I'd gladly watch that zombie tear you apart. Hell, I'd let it have its way with me so long as I get to watch you go first."

The chief stepped closer and cocked his head with a sick amusement. "Assuming you were what you said you were, are you so foolhardy you believe there are no worse things out there? Let me tell you a little something about this golem. You see, it has these hoses, and they're built right into it, like an extra set of arms, and they're capped with these hollow spikes. If it helps, think of them like giant syringes or needles, and do you know what it uses them for?"

"I've heard all this, and I don't care. You're not scaring me," Pyles responded.

"Yeah, I am," Lawson replied. "Because that thing is going to be quick to attack, and you will be slow to die. You haven't seen the aftermath of its feeding, but I have. I've watched the EMTs scrape the remains of my friend in the store off a hardwood floor. The golem uses those feeding tubes while it hold you like a fly caught in a web. Imagine a big fella like you being as helpless as a kitten as those hoses sink into your veins. Do you understand? It drinks you like lemonade on a hot day, and that's not even the most gruesome part. You see, it wants every drop and will mash your organs. Mash them until they're nothing but a pulp-filled goop." The chief made several slurping noises and jammed two fingers into the crook of his arm, like a junkie shooting up.

"For all your talk, you might be the one to go," Pyles said.

"Maybe," Lawson said, dismissing this with a wave. "But you'll go before me, one way or another."

A short echoing scream turned all of them to the empty corridor. Several gunshots proceeded a horrible cry for help. The temperature plummeted as their breath hung in the air. The room gained an unexpected chill, as if someone had opened a window to early January. The Fogies experienced a powerful rush of the ether, instilling in them a strange sort of serenity.

Pyles whispered, "It's the jar. Someone is using it."

"Wadim," Bronagh said.

Chief Lawson stepped away from the hall and further into the room as a thick, billowing fog followed. The wall of impenetrable mist pursued Lawson like a hungry predator, snapping at his heels.

Lawson bellowed, "Whoever you are, just know I am not without power."

The chief cracked his neck and revealed it to be covered with more scales. His forked tongue lapped at the chilled air as his eyes took on a strange glow. Lawson used his gun to smash the lightbulb next to him, putting a large shadow over the room.

The mist rolled in like smoke caught in a high wind, and in its folds, came a flicker of movement. A human shape stirred within the cloud before vanishing once more into the haze.

"Officer Cook, is that you?" Lawson shouted.

He moved into the darkened corner and raised his pistol toward the fog. His prayers came like rambling whispers as the unholy gleam from his eyes intensified.

The fog continued flowing into the room, forcing Lawson further back into his corner. He put a shaky grasp on his radio and said, "This is Lawson. Dispatch, tell me you copy."

His answer came as a static that broke into the beeps of whatever dialer had been trying to carry the signal of his radio. He took in a steadying breath and said again, "Whoever is manning the radios had better answer…this is Lawson. Goddamn it, this is Lawson."

A bloody Officer Cook collapsed out of the fog. The glossy gaze she wore said she was dead before her skull cracked on the stone floor. Her throat had been ripped out and her shirt was little more than a bloodied mess. Lawson observed his fallen comrade, but offered no assistance. He raised the gun and didn't have to wait long as something exited the mist in a terrifying rush.

A vampiric-looking Wadim emerged, holding the jar under one clawed hand. With the other, he reached for the horrified Lawson. The chief fired his gun with several well-aimed hits. The bullets ripped through the vampiric Wadim, but he refused to stop. One of the shots tore a peephole into his jaw, exposing the razor-sharp fangs underneath, and still he continued.

The chief's years of experience and maybe some demonic influence kept his hands from faltering. Every shot he fired found its target, ripping away most of Wadim's mouth and a corner of his skull.

"Why won't you die already?" Lawson growled, as Wadim ripped the gun away.

Wadim tried to speak, but his words came out as mush. Already the jar and his recent feedings were working on putting him back together.

Lawson screamed and threw a solid punch with all his weight behind it. Wadim, however, stepped past the blow. He moved up to the chief's ear as if to share a secret. His jaw unhinged, and with the wide mouth of a shark, Wadim bit his way through the struggling chief's neck.

Pyles and Bronagh didn't see much of what followed. They could hear, though, and the gnawing eventually turned to a slurping, and finally, some brief time later, a satisfied smacking of the lips.

Pyles fanned the air and said, "I'm happy to see you. How did you find us?"

A sound like teeth gnashing bone came from the corner where Wadim continued his meal. "The blood called to me from the parking lot."

"Wadim…uh…thanks and all," Pyles said. "Can you say something? You're freaking us out over here."

Wadim stood and dragged an arm across his mouth. He slammed a heavy claw into what remained of the chief's head until something, possibly the jawbone, cracked like thin ice.

Wadim said, "Just a moment. I want to make sure this terrible individual does not come back, like in the horror movies."

Pyles shook his still shackled leg. "Don't go to crazy, because one of them has the key."

Bronagh tried to look away from the carnage. "Oh, Wadim…what have you done? There is bad, very bad."

Wadim lingered in the shadows, his eyes carrying a red glint to them, his face a floating horror in the darkness. "I have fed and fed well. I am strong enough now to bend the metal that holds you."

"Thanks, but I'd prefer having these things off the old-fashioned way," Pyles replied.

In the gloom, Wadim's skin had lost some of the wrinkles as well as some color. Under the sway of the jar, his flesh resembled wax paper. The dye from his re-forming skull and hair ran like India ink between sharp teeth crowded too close together.

"Never mind. I can reach that female cop's boot, if I stretch. She's the one who put us in these things. I bet she still has the key," Pyles said.

He hunched over and landed a loose grip on the dead officer's foot. Pyles yanked, and the body came across the floor in pieces. He turned his head from the remains and fished the key out her shirt pocket. His stomach lurched at the smell, but swallowing helped, and the urge passed.

Pyles worked on shackles and as soon as they were off, he did the same for Bronagh. Freed from their chains, they came together around Conole's body. Wadim joined, displaying the gleeful sneer of a madman, almost mirroring the same expressions the chief and his lackeys had shown.

"After everything we've seen and done, it ends like this for him…no worse tragedy than a great life cut short," Pyles said, choking back what he would never admit were tears.

Bronagh bowed her head and found the mountain man's wrist across the distance of her own grief. They joined hands like kids crossing the street together.

Bronagh wept and reached to stroke Conole's hair. She pushed a stray lock away from his brow and caressed the nape of his neck. "I never told him how much I cared. In all the time I knew him, he never asked for more than I was willing to give. Like me, he didn't get to have a mom and dad. We didn't get to have a childhood to teach us right from wrong. But somehow, he still managed to represent everything good about mortality and innocence."

Pyles sniffled and said, "Amen to that. He was a better man than I, but I don't reckon we had to tell him. Conole knew, and he did his best to try to help us get there."

Bronagh glanced up to see Wadim creeping toward them with his fangs barred. She squeezed Pyles's hand and held him beside her. "Wadim, is this how you want to say good-bye to our friend? Or perhaps you would like to lap his blood up off the floor?"

Her words were low, but carried the force to stop Wadim dead in his tracks. If it was possible for a monster to show shame, their vampire friend wore the expression like a mask. Wadim put the jar down and pried his grip away from the lid. This separation stopped the wave of the ether and ended his transformation. His humanity returned, but the wrinkles of his skin didn't stretch as far, and a snatch of natural charcoal black appeared in his hair. Not an oily dye or a cheap tinting job, but the real color he'd said good-bye to around his fiftieth birthday.

Wadim settled back into humanity with a final shiver. He crossed his arms over his chest and said, "My apologies. The change made me not care as much. It detached me from having to accept what those sadists did. I wanted to stay that way forever. I knew this would hurt, losing him like this. I see now what those animals did and would have done to you had they not been stopped."

"That is what makes it so dangerous," Bronagh whispered. She put her free hand into Wadim's, and each of the Fogies silently said good-bye to their friend.

"Conole, my brother, my companion, if this thing really granted wishes, you would be standing 8' tall beside us right now," Wadim said.

Bronagh swayed on her feet, the heaviness of loss pulling on her to the point of near collapse. Through will alone, she remained upright. "Conole, where you lay is soft, and where you go bright. Either in this world or the next, we'll meet again."

Pyles pounded his chest where the hitches made it tough to speak his piece. "Bud, you were a decent guy whose word I would have taken even if you told me you could pee out your finger. It isn't much, but where I'm from there's no bigger compliment. Rest easy. We'll shoulder the rest of the load from here. You rest yourself for a bit."

Bronagh lowered her chin until it touched her chest like a sleeping bird. "Let's give it a moment, and bow our heads. I can't ask you to pray, but I can request the minute of silence given to honor Conole, our brother."

Wadim and Pyles did as Bronagh asked, and however brief the silence lasted, none of them wanted it to end. Then the urgency of everything that had happened and could still happen cut into their mourning. They were surrounded by dead bodies in the satanic subbasement of a building still presumably full of police. There were fingerprints to consider and the fact that half the precinct no doubt knew who they were and where they lived. This meant they weren't simply the prime suspects, but the *only* suspects.

Pyles gritted his teeth and kicked the chief's dead body until Bronagh stopped him. She had to drag him back to the group and once done, Pyles said, "They're going to pin this whole mess on us, and hang everyone we know from the highest tree. I count two dead assholes and a saint, and that's not considering any of the other jag offs Wadim might have fed on. They'll fry us for this."

Wadim nudged the jar with his shoe. "I admit it; this thing has been nothing but trouble. We can't leave it here, though. We can't leave it here for these ne'er-do-wells to use. Something must be done, but I don't know what."

Bronagh had found one of Conole's small shoes and held it in her hand. She clutched the thing like a safety blanket. "We'll take it somewhere and smash it into a thousand pieces. Let them try to use it then."

"But first we need to get out of here." Wadim pulled the chief's shirt off and used it to prepare the jar for travel. The deputy's belt acted as a fine rope to secure the ripped fabric, but a large portion of the glass bottom was still uncovered.

Pyles went to scout out the situation in the corridor and came rushing back a minute later. "There's another dead cop by the door, and the head is missing. I have a suspicion it landed outside. Wadim, is it outside? You know what? Don't answer."

"Honestly, I don't recall," Wadim replied.

Bronagh continued clutching Conole's shoe. She wiped at her nose and said, "What about Conole? We can't leave him down here. Will one of you carry him out?"

"I have another idea," Wadim said. He turned to Bronagh and Pyles and held up the jar. "We don't know touching it won't bring him back. You saw what it did to my wounds. There can't be any harm in trying."

Bronagh stepped between Conole's body and Wadim's approach. She shook her head and looked ready to fight if need be. "No, don't you come near him with that cursed thing. It tempts us with what we want, but brings nothing but pain. I'll not see it perverse him."

"You're emotionally bothered, and I won't tell you how to feel, but you are denying our comrade a possible resurrection," Wadim said, touching the top of the jar either by choice or because he couldn't help himself.

Bronagh didn't like the addict-like qualities Wadim displayed toward the glass. She couldn't remember him being a pacer before, but now he walked a short back-and-forth around the jar. He had become a jittery mess when not near it.

Bronagh stood her ground and said, "Do you recall the fable about the monkey's paw? I can't explain it, but I feel it in my bones that whatever that thing in the glass might do for Conole, it wouldn't be good."

Wadim, still looking and sounding younger, replied, "That was a story, not a fable. You don't want to take the chance. Fine, so be it, but this conversation is on hiatus. It is not done by any stretch of the imagination."

Pyles whistled to get their attention. "You're like two construction workers arguing about who's going first at the shitter. Hell, you're not even sure there's going to be toilet paper inside. Can we please get a move on?"

Pyles rummaged around the bodies and came up with the female officer's car keys. He shook them and said, "Has anyone thought about how we're getting home, because they're not going to let us on the bus with a body?"

Wadim unbuttoned the female deputy's shirt and passed it to a disgusted-looking Pyles. "Here, cover Conole with this. You carry him to the unmarked car I left in the parking lot. I'll use the ether to clear the way."

Pyles tried to hold the shredded shirt by the unblemished corners of the sleeves. "How did you do that with the mist? That was you, right?"

Wadim put a finger against the glass, and in response, his nail thickened to a pronounced point. "The more I'm exposed to it, the more I figure out and remember. Given enough time, I think I'll be able to bring people over, and the change will be permanent…I hope so, anyway."

Bronagh aided in covering Conole and whispered, "No more about jars and changing anyone. I'm ready to get out of this hellhole."

Pyle's scooped up Conole's remains, and they moved into the corridor. Wadim took the lead and kept the jar in a bear hug just above his exposed belly. This made it so a single hard breath could bring the two together.

They traveled along the subbasement of the building and the eerie silence suggested the exploration of an endless catacomb. Bronagh, Wadim, and Pyles followed the stone hall to the corpse-laden exit. The remains of the third deputy lay smashed against the metal doorframe where Wadim had left him. The statement about the missing head had proven to be true.

"My word, Wadim," Bronagh said. She looked to Wadim for an explanation for his actions, but he could only shrug.

"This could be our Butch and Sundance end," Pyles said, shifting the weight of Conole from one shoulder to the other as he peeked outside. "We go through this door, and every swinging pecker in a blue uniform could be lined up waiting to blow us away. I'm saying this so you guys understand I got no regrets about biting the big one in such company."

Wadim approached the door leading out of the basement and used the toe of his shoe to wedge it open. "Hate to ruin your cowboy moment, Hopalong, but I don't see anyone. Some of the cars are missing, though. There were two squad cars parked by the steps. I don't see either one now."

Wadim opened the door a little wider and counted to ten before giving his friends the thumbs-up of everything being okay. They made it to the unmarked car Wadim had taken without incident.

"I don't like this," Bronagh said. "It's as though they sensed what happened and fled like scalded dogs."

Pyles studied the street to make sure none of the remaining police were lurking about the shadows. "Could be the ones in the basement with us were the ring leaders, and now with them gone, the others don't know what to do."

Wadim growled, "We would be wise not to question to our stroke of good fortune. We should be away from here."

Bronagh still held Conole's shoe like her own talisman. She looked at it and at Conole's body. "Let's go home."

They briefly bickered about where to put Conole, but Pyles settled the debate on his own. He went around to the rear of the car and hammered on the trunk. "From here on out, we're playing this as low-key as humanly possible. I loved Conole like a brother, but I doubt he would have cared. Now open the trunk up already, 'cause he's not riding up there. New rule: No dead bodies in the car with us."

Pyles lowered Conole into the trunk and gave his departed friend a gentle punch to the chest. The painful parting might have lasted longer, but Wadim started the unmarked cruiser and almost backed over a curb. In a rush, Pyles had to jog to get into the car.

"You almost ditched me, asshole," Pyles yelled as they bounced onto the sidewalk and cut across a parking lot.

Wadim switched on the local police bandwidth on the radio and said, "No one enjoys the company of a backseat driver."

Pyles replied, "Our first order of business is we ditch this cruiser in the woods by my trailer. Then we call a cab to take us to our vehicles, and from there, it's a mass exodus out of this shithole. See you in the funny papers."

"No," Bronagh said, touching the scabbed-over cut on her cheek from the fire. She picked at it until fresh blood tricked along her skin. When her fingers were covered, she used the blood to mark Conole's shoe. "There's something else we have to do, and somewhere else we have to go."

Wadim turned sharply onto the main drag and drove straight through a stoplight. "What are you talking about, dear? My patience has run its course for mystery. We may be suspects in a fire and a murder. That zombie of theirs may be hunting us right now. I agree with Pyles. Time to consider a change of locations."

"Here, here," Pyles cheered.

Wadim scanned the different police bands for any mention of the chaos behind them, but found nothing.

"Someone should have noticed something by now. I wonder if this was not some side effect of our friend in the jar. We know it affects everyone a bit differently. I have an idea that it could be our demonic friend might be responsible for this lull. As if those in the building have spaced out like the people at Bronagh's complex."

"Pull over," Bronagh whispered, her voice carrying a level of distress that suggested a sudden illness.

"This isn't really the best time for this," Wadim replied.

"Pull over," Bronagh said once more.

Pyles stared out the back windshield as if searching for possible pursuers. "This isn't really the most ideal moment or place for this. Maybe we could wait till we're home,"

Bronagh dipped into the inside of her blouse and removed the deputy's gun from where she'd hid it. While exiting the police station, she had seen the smaller caliber pistol in a leg holster of the headless body. Pyles and Wadim were too worried about escaping to take notice.

The gun grabbed their attention, and Bronagh pointed it at the floorboards as if she intended to shoot through the floor. "Lads, I hate having to repeat myself. I'll say this one more time. Put the cruiser over there by that guardrail so we can talk. I want everyone's undivided attention for what I have to say."

Wadim sneered, "You felt the need to draw a gun? Very well, please keep your finger away from the firing mechanism."

"Trigger," Pyles replied. "It's called a 'trigger.' Easy, old gal. It don't take much, and that thing doesn't have a safety. You mess around, and you'll end up blowing your foot off."

Wadim tapered off the gas and turned the cruiser onto the empty roadside. He grumbled in what could have been fine gibberish or rushed Romanian. "I'm going, I'm going, but what is so vital it can't be hatched over while we're escaping Satanic police?"

Pyles said, "Bronagh, have you lost your mind to be waving that piece around in here? I want to believe this is grief madness, but gal, Wadim isn't kidding about escape. We need to go like post, posthaste."

With the car finally stopped, a silence came over them. The woods were dark, and the night swarmed with bugs. In the distance, they could still hear the occasional vehicle zoom past. The stars had come out as if to shine on their tiny spot in the universe. Crickets chirped, and clouds of gnats danced in the light of the moon.

Bronagh turned the gun over in her palm like a rosary. She closed both hands over it, as if wanting to swear an oath upon the metal and bullets. The blood from her reopened wound smeared the barrel, turning it red.

Bronagh alternated between touching the gun and Conole's shoe. "Thank you, Wadim, for the daring rescue. You saved us from some terrible end. You and Pyles have done much and suffered loss same as I have. I shouldn't ask any more of you, but there might not be a choice. First, tell me—do you believe what they said about their golem? Do you think it will come for us and the jar, no matter what?"

"I do," Pyles said, without hesitation, showing himself wrestling with the same grim conclusion. "That thing in the jar, even if it is dead, is pulling strings and using that zombie like a puppet. Yes, I have no doubt it will come."

Wadim tried the police scanner again and still found nothing. He put his head to the steering well and fell into a deliberate silence.

Bronagh squeezed Wadim's shoulder and drew no response. She looked to Pyles, and he could only shrug.

Bronagh said, "If you're blaming yourself, you should stop. None of us could have seen this happening. But we can stop it from going any further. I know it may be asking a great deal, but we can't just throw the jar away. If the zombie can sense it, nowhere is far enough or safe enough. I've been mulling the problem over, and I've concluded destroying the jar might be a very bad idea. We're like people stumbling upon an old war weapon, and in fact, that's exactly what we've done. We don't know what the repercussions or effects might be. It could release something like a contagion that will spread unabated. Sad truth is…this jar is our cross to bear, and somehow, we must finish this."

Wadim beat his head on the steering wheel. Not with any real force, but hard enough he beeped the horn once. He surprised the other two with a short chuckle after being startled by the sudden noise.

Pyles stroked his bead and said, "I'm too old to be the cowboy hero. Too old to be fighting monsters and wrestling with demon babies. Bronagh, I don't know what we can to do stop this thing. You heard the cops; it even had them spooked, and they had an entire police force. What do we have?"

"Hope," Bronagh replied. "Compassion, the things they gave up when they began consorting with the dark. The things that jar would strip from us if we allowed it to truly give us the immortality I thought I wanted."

"Say what you want, but I'm always the boss of me," Pyles growled. "It's a great speech, but none of this is going to help."

Wadim turned to them, beaming a wide grin. His skin still looked rejuvenated from his prolonged exposure to the jar. His eyes had regained some luster of youth. He still wasn't a young man, but it looked as though his odometer had been rolled back a couple of birthdays. He pointed to the empty spot in the backseat where Conole would have been sitting normally.

"Back there, I was lost in the ether, awash with power and didn't care one iota my friend had passed. I saw his body and the vampiric me felt nothing. I couldn't mourn our brother then, but I mourn him now. That jar tried to take what I had in my heart for him, and for all of you, and it did its best to destroy it. Bah, I say, bah to the jar and this golem. Conole is not here to say Bronagh is right, someone must do something. So I will say it for him. If not us, then who? Who else is in the position to do something?"

Pyles looked to empty spot in the backseat and clenched his jaw to maybe hold off tears. "Conole would have said it better, but you're not wrong. For him, I'll chew this thing's head off and crap down its throat."

"Then we are in agreement," Wadim said.

Bronagh faced the darkness ahead of them and hoped they were making the right decision. The question had been asked and still not answered about what could they do to the thing? The answer escaped her, and despite the rousing words, she hoped she hadn't set them on a fool's errand.

Chapter 18

When they drove up to the ball field, no one was thinking about Cracker Jacks, popcorn, or rooting for the home team. Instead, the remaining Fogies tried to ignore the ether Wadim's caressing of the glass released. He spaced out the light contact to follow along with the mile markers as they laid their trail. He had maintained a willingness to give up the jar's power, but his obsession with it worried Bronagh and Pyles. The two exchanged concerned glances, but said nothing of the addiction.

By the time the Fogies parked the cruiser beneath the away-side bleachers, Pyles had been forced to take over as the driver. Wadim couldn't focus on resisting the change and steering. So he slipped into the backseat beside the jar and surrendered the keys. He cupped the jar like a sick pet, and even whispered quiet lullabies as the road jostled the car.

"How long do you figure we have before everything goes to shit?" Pyles asked as they gazed across the painted diamond, marking the bases.

"I doubt it will be very long," Wadim said. "I can feel something in the air. I believe the golem is coming, but what will happen after that is anyone's guess."

Pyles pointed at Bronagh. "You're starting to sound like her."

"Yeah," Wadim said with a grin. "It is indeed crazy, but come, we have things to prepare, and I will not be caught with my pants unfastened."

They found the lock-covered fuse box controlling the lights. and after touching the jar, Pyles had the strength to tear it open. They had agreed it was best to share the responsibility of using the fetus, and Pyles took his turn. He flipped the breaker for the scoreboard lights, and the field became a bright beacon in the liquid blackness of the night.

Meanwhile, Wadim went to the open tool shed and took stock of everything inside. He counted two long handed shovels, a few banged-up weed eaters, and a lawn mower old enough to be considered an antique. He tossed the shovels over by the dugout and dragged a garden hose over to the home plate. The Fogies had an idea to use fire, but the logistics of how remained mostly unanswered. The hose would act as a preventive measure against igniting the country.

Pyles showed Bronagh how to properly hold the pistol and how to fire. "Easy pulls," he said. "You'll get less recoil that way."

Bronagh gripped the gun and practiced holding it steady. Her arms trembled no matter how she positioned herself. Eventually she offered the weapon to Pyles. "You should take it. I'm as likely to shoot one of you as anything else."

Pyles examined her technique or lack thereof and agreed. He moved to take the gun, but lingered at the touch of her wrist against his. He allowed himself a touch of her elbow.

Wadim's face reddened as he watched. He swallowed hard and yelled, "We do not have the spare seconds for physical engagements. My dear comrades, the clock is indeed ticking away."

The piercing cold of the ether punctured the summer heat as Pyles moved the jar to the corner of the fence. Before the change could overtake him, he stepped away from the fetus. He stared off into the dark woods beyond the reach of the lights, momentarily overwhelmed by a raw stink.

"I smell something," Pyles yelled. "The stink caught me off guard, but it's strong enough to water my eyes. The wind must have been blowing the other way before, but my god, is it rank."

Wadim peered into the gloom beyond the light's glow and said, "I do not see anything." He snatched the jar and proceeded into the dark. "I shall end this myself, so no more innocent blood shall be spilled."

"Wait up…you idiot, wait," Pyles yelled. They had devised a rough plan in the car and so far, none of it had happened as it was supposed to.

Ahead of Bronagh and Pyles, an energized Wadim glided across the dry ground to the woods where Pyles had pointed. Wadim, fully immersed as a vampire, vanished into the dark, and his friends could only pursue him past the safety of the lights. Bronagh used the small glow of a penlight she'd found in the cruiser to brighten their path as Pyles pushed after Wadim's scent.

They came upon the source of the stink near a fallen tree. Wadim had released his grip on the glass and looked to his friends for an explanation of the strange mosaic carnage he had discovered. The horrific scene shook them all.

Around the fallen log, some soulless thing had torn a pregnant doe to pieces and used the parts to create a sculpture to depravity. A litter of dead bugs marked the ichor sprayed across the tree bark as the golem's residue, its brackish blood.

Bronagh spun away from the grizzly monument. "It's here or was here."

"This is sick…like real sick," Pyles said, covering his mouth and nose with his shirt. "Why the hell would it do this?"

Wadim dared to touch the pile of gore and said, "Could be it came here when we buried the jar, but arrived after I had already taken it. This seems like something a frustrated psychopath does."

Bronagh put her penlight away, and Wadim belched to try and lull a rampaging stomach. He kicked the log until the propped-up deer limbs collapsed into the brush.

"Mindless things don't do something like this," Bronagh said. "This is evil, pure evil."

Pyles bolted back to the field and made it to the foul line before he spat up a throatful of stomach acid. Wadim clutched the jar again and walked the other two back to the visitors' dugout. They looked around but saw nothing of the monster, and Pyles couldn't sniff it out over the deer carcass.

Bronagh tried to catch her breath and said, "Remember what we discussed. I think there was a gas can in cruiser's trunk. Let's hope it's not empty."

Chapter 19

While they all heard the crashing of the trees, Wadim saw the golem first. The great commotion didn't fall in with the man-sized creature they were expecting. The heavy crash of dry lumber being snapped and maybe even exploded seemed to signal the coming of an industrial-sized steamroller—a steel casted nightmare capable of flattening everything in its path as it tore a swath across the land.

Wadim, not by accident, happened to be closest to the fetus when the noise began. He reached out for the ether and surrendered to the change. His predatory gaze picked up the movement of the golem's far-stretching hoses whipping wildly through the woods destroying, desecrating, and filleting anything possibly slowing its progress to the fetus.

Wadim took the jar under his arm and stepped to the front of their tiny formation. "It's coming. We must be ready. Its tubes are strong and unbelievably agile. It will be like fighting a human spider."

"Let me try a few rounds with this pistol before you go tussling with it," Pyles said. He checked the sights of the police-grade weapon and aimed toward the center of the noise.

Bronagh stood behind a pair of shovels jammed into the earth of the pitcher's mound. In the shed she had found an old orange dust rag and used it to tie her hair up. The look wasn't going to win her any modeling contracts, but at different points both Pyles and Wadim had promised themselves to be the one to pull off her when everything was finally over.

"Do not let it get any of its gunk on you either," Bronagh shouted.

"Wait," Wadim said, taking a few small steps forward. "It stopped moving. I've lost it behind the trees."

"Let me get a look," Pyles replied. He tucked the pistol under his shirt and put a hand onto the glass.

For the first time two of them dared touch the jar at once. Like the times before, thick fur sprang up and ran like an untamed river over Pyles's exposed skin. His clothes and belongings disappeared into the emerging beast.

"The…whole…woods…smells like…it," he said before his vocal cords produced only snarling grunts.

The Fogies held their breaths in a quiet hush, but didn't have to wait long before an uprooted tree came hurtling out of the night. The Fogies had a split second to panic before the heavy elm tree's impact.

Wadim reacted fast enough to avoid being hit, but this caused him to inadvertently rip the jar away from Pyles. The tree struck the now-human mountain man and pinned him to the ground in an explosion of bark and wood.

Wadim, vampire or not, did have the forethought to pull Bronagh out of harm's way. Her wrist popped in the vampire's grip, and she could hear Pyles's screams from underneath the uprooted tree.

"My leg, it's crushed. I can't move it." Pyles whimpered.

Bronagh forgot all about the gas can, the gun, and even the golem as she heard the distress and rising pain in her friend's cries. "Pyles, wait there. Don't try to move; I'm coming."

"No," Wadim said, restraining her by the elbow. He didn't have to elaborate as to why. At the peak of this chaos, the golem appeared at the border of the outfield.

Like a Tinkertoy designed by H. R. Geiger, the machine-like undead horror marched forward on legs covered by battered and torn canvas pants. Holes in the cloth revealed bulging metallic knees that moved like pistons. Its once-human chest had been affixed with a rusty metal plate bolted into the sternum. From behind the plate came a low whirling sound, like some unseen engine coming to life. The golem's mouth had been sewn shut into a horrific caricature of a smile. Endlessly the monster stared through sunken, lidless eyes with the sick likeness of rotted, deflated fruit.

A pair of long rubber hoses capped with silver needles ran out of its exposed back and acted as extra appendages. To Bronagh, Pyles, and Wadim's horror, the hoses shot forward to the ground and pulled the golem along like some nightmarish marionette.

"Saints preserve us," Bronagh said as Wadim took hold of one of the shovels and waved it at the approaching monster.

Pyles tried to shimmy out from under the tree. He did so at the cost of wrenching on a shinbone already twisted like the salted pretzels they served in a concession stand.

"Pull me out, pull me out," Pyles moaned. He reached for the pistol, but in the fall, it had tumbled over between second and third base.

Bronagh managed to break free of Wadim's hold. She brought the other shovel over to act as a lever under the tree as she tried to pry Pyles loose. The tree rocked in place and rolled up, allowing Pyles to rescue his mutilated shin, but when it slipped back it did so on his ankle. Pyles shrieked and clawed at tree pinning him in place.

"Wadim, you have to help me," Bronagh yelled.

Wadim heard her, because his head turned slightly, but he never slowed in his chosen course. He raised the long-handled shovel and met the first of the golem's hoses in mid attack.

Wadim successfully deflected the hose and needle, though he gained no ground. Up close, he could see the hoses ended in large hypodermics dripping the black ichor the residue of its feeding, he figured. Like a two-way pump, the hoses took the blood in and expelled the ichor like refuse.

Wadim circled the golem, jabbing with the shovel as it neared. "I don't know if you can understand. Nor do I even really care, but you'll have to pry this jar out of my dead fingers. Do you hear me, you kraut piece of crap?"

Wadim spun the spade in a circle and kept the jar over the hip furthest away from the fight. The moves weren't executed with any kind of skill, and yet they held the golem and its snakelike hoses at bay.

Bronagh tried to move the log again, but one of the roots on the other side kept acting as a kickstand. She took the shovel and set about removing the problem, trying to forget about what was happening in the outfield. Bronagh hacked until finally when she tried to lever it again, the tree rolled off the now unconscious Pyles.

"Come on, this is no time for a nap. You need to wake up, Pyles. It's coming this way," Bronagh said. She noticed where the gun had fallen and picked it up.

Even with his supernatural speed, the pair of hoses kept Wadim on the back foot. He miscalculated an attack, and the golem shot a hand out and wrenched the shovel away.

This distraction allowed one of the needles to embed itself in Wadim's chest. The excruciating pain would have killed a normal person. The supernatural Wadim fought to remove the needle and felt it syphoning his blood into the golem.

The hose coiled before lashing out to flick him and the jar across the field. Wadim lost his grip on the fetus and could only lie there and moan as he connected with the hard ground. The jar came to rest near the infield, miraculously still intact.

Bronagh had to do something as both her friends lay dying. She dashed to the jar and used the hem of her skirt to roll the glass over to Pyles. She directed it to his bare neck where the pulse had started to fade.

"It's still coming," Wadim yelled. He held his insides together and crawled after the glass. He stopped when Bronagh fired the gun.

Bronagh bit her lip and raised the pistol. She rattled off shots at the golem like Pyles had showed her. Having never handled a gun before, she managed to put a round into its shoulder. The bullet glanced off the thing's metallic underneath and caused it to pause for a moment.

The large wolf-man Pyles came to his feet, cradling the jar. With a roar, he charged the golem. Like a mad bull the giant wolf ignored the stabs of the hoses even as the silver capped needles burned through his skin. He pushed past the pain and slammed into the golem, knocking them both over.

The golem righted itself with the aid of the extra appendages, but Pyles was there, waiting. His powerful jaws wrenched on the golem's injured shoulder and a metallic crunch ripped through the night. This blow sent the golem backward, but left an opening for the hoses to puncture deep into the wolf's body. The blood flowed, and a spray of black gunk erupted out of the golem's back as it fed on the weakening Pyles.

Bronagh gripped the gun and focused on finding the golem at the end of it. Bronagh pulled the trigger in a single, fluid tug. The gun flashed, and the corner of the golem's head rocked back enough to allow Pyles to escape.

Even in his animal state, Pyles still had the good sense to know when to retreat. The silver-tipped needles had nearly killed him. Another few moments of fighting and the injuries would have been fatal.

Pyles used his nimbleness to roll away, giving Bronagh the open space to fire again. She squeezed off a trio of shots and hit the golem twice in the chest, causing it to turn its blank stare on her. The third shot went wide, and she wondered how long before the gun would click empty.

In all his efforts to evade the silver needles, Pyles lost his grip on the jar and his wounds along with his strength dissipated. He looked about like a lost child, not sure where to go.

He scrambled to get his hands around the glass, but the golem and its terrible reach made it there first. It hoses wrapped around the jar and delivered the glass to its outstretched arms. As soon as the two were reunited, the rawest ocean of the ether erupted across the land. The energy engulfed everything nearby in an invisible bubble of body-shuddering gratification, blurring the lines of pleasure and pain.

The energy carried a taint now like the bitter aftertaste of suddenly soured fruit. The corruption seemed to spread and gentle tingles became biting pinches. On the outside, the golem manifested changes as well As if rewinding time itself, the sunken, shriveled eye pits became perfect bowls of creamy white milk, carrying the roundest brown center of a pupil. The golem's desiccated skin revived and resembled a slick and water-beaded seal hide.

With the jar raised high, the golem tore open the stiches of its mouth to produce an ear-piercing whine. In this nightmarish moment, the thing within the jar, the demonic fetus, moved.

Chapter 20

The stirrings at first seemed to come from the shifting of the fetus's glass prison, but then Bronagh and a retreating Pyles watched the tiny leather wings unfurl themselves with a flutter. After this, there could be no mistaking the twisting of its horned head and the small shriek as it screamed like a hungry newborn. This miraculous resurrection released the biggest wave of energy yet.

Energy from the other side and pain ran free like an electric pulse. The unchecked ether rolled the muscles up into knotted, binding cramps and sucked every ounce of warmth out of the skin. From inside the jar came a screech so loud and piercing it lingered in the eardrums.

Bronagh noticed a splintering in the side of the glass. A second later, the crack arced into a small fissure going underneath the bottom of the jar. The hellion, still temporarily contained, put a single pushpin-sized claw into space, and worked for its freedom.

Pyles had crawled-ran enough to reach Bronagh. Though he had surrendered his supernatural strength, he had also surrendered all but the most minor injuries. He looked to be nursing a sprained wrist, but despite the pain, the mountain man pulled Bronagh to the fence marking the outfield.

"We have to go. This is finished. There's nothing else we can do," he said.

Bronagh stopped at the fence and resisted his insistence that she climb over the top to the parking lot. "Where's Wadim?" she asked, causing them both to look around for their missing friend. He wasn't anywhere on the field, and Pyles caught the headlights of the cruiser come on as the car came squealing toward them.

"He asked for the keys back while we were in the shed. I thought he wanted to feel important since I had the jar," Pyles said, momentarily caught in the glare of the headlights. He snatched the gas can and dashed for his life

"Run," Bronagh yelled, as the car accelerated in their direction.

Bronagh tripped over something in the grass, but Pyles caught her arms. They watched as Wadim, behind the wheel of the cruiser, knocked the fence down and raced onto the field.

Bronagh made it to the home team's bench without needing to jump. Pyles, though, had to leap as if he was going for a gold medal. His hold on the gas can complicated his landing. The thumb on his right hand absorbed a lot of the impact of his body with a loud snap. Pyles shrieked and pushed the can to Bronagh.

Wadim had spun the car around in the outfield and had it speeding straight at the golem. The golem wrestled to keep hold of the jar as the glass cracked up to the lid. At the last moment before impact, the hoses, like angels descending from heaven, pulled the golem out of harm's way, causing the cruiser to shoot past.

Inside the cruiser, Wadim turned hard on the wheel until the car almost collided with the scoreboard. He righted the wheels and mashed on the gas for a second run. This set him and the beast once again on a collision course. Bronagh and Pyles could only watch from the safety of the dugout.

Wadim shouted something about roadkill and perspective before the pair of hoses shot through the windshield. They obliterated the interior of the cruiser but snagged themselves in the wire cage. This mistake enabled the reinforced grill of the car to accelerate directly into the metal and flesh of the trapped golem.

The hit sent the golem across the hood and into the remnants of the windshield. The cruiser turned and came careening straight for the corner of the fence beside Bronagh and Pyles.

They had a second to choose a course of action before the car struck the dugout with the force of a miniature explosion. Pyles shoved Bronagh out of the impact zone, and she landed on the grass amidst a spray of broken glass and metal. Her bones groaned in protest, and she knew there would be bruising and much swelling if she survived.

Bronagh tried to call for Wadim and Pyles, but the ensuing screech of what must have been the demon spawn trying free itself drowned her out. The power short-circuited the lights and plunged the field into darkness. The air held the stink of smoke and burning metal, and a small fire had worked its way up from one of the overturned cruisers tires.

The wind buffeted her with a stream of black smoke, caused by the burning rubber. The cruiser had flipped over on its side and the front end was wedged into the concrete foundation of the dugout. The trunk had come open in the crash, but Conole's body was nowhere to be seen. It might have been funny to worry about a dead friend while a pair of living ones needed her, but Bronagh's mind ran in a circle, and she had to let it catch up.

Something moved in the wreckage, and from the shattered back windshield a scratched-covered Wadim crawled free. He groaned and muttered until his shoes touched the ground. He crawled like a drunk to the grass and rolled onto his back. He coughed to clear his throat and spat blood at the wreckage.

Bronagh kneeled beside him and took his head into her lap. "You're okay. You're going to be okay. But I don't see Pyles anywhere."

Upon waking to her, Wadim wept and kissed the palm stroking his brow. "I love you, ye gods, how I love you. I don't want to die without you knowing how I feel. How I've always felt about you. My life or un-life is meaningless without you."

"I know," Bronagh said. "Now is maybe not the time to discuss this." She looked to the wreckage and spied the lid of the glass container lying against the oil pan. Something darted under the hood away from a growing blaze of flaming wreckage. She had dropped the gun in her haste to escape, and it had vanished somewhere underneath the overturned car.

Bronagh said, "Did you see Pyles? What did you do with Conole's body?"

"Pyles? No, I haven't seen him. I put Conole by the road. I'm sorry; I didn't want to disrespect his remains."

Bronagh called to Pyles and left Wadim so she could scour the crash site. She ventured as close as the heat would allow and prayed Pyles would reveal himself alive and well. She heard a scuttling noise and the crunching of glass, but no sign of either the mountain man or wolf.

The car shifted as the hood collapsed and a part of the bumper came away a moment before the hoses tore a path up through the engine. Like the great beast Leviathan rising from revelations, the golem tore itself free of the debris.

The impact had revealed a piece of the monster's skull and one of its legs didn't look as if it bent correctly. This injury caused a hitch as it moved. Its eyes once again resembling deflated fruit, focused on Bronagh. Slowly the golem moved toward her.

Wadim somehow made it to his feet and put himself between Bronagh and the thing. He leaned upon her and raised a threatening fist. "Come any further, and I'll teach you a thing or two about drinking blood. Siphon some of mine, and I'll do my best to give you indigestion."

The ear-piercing scream of the demon child came again, but something cut it off mid-shriek. What followed sounded like a shrill, inhuman wail of pain. This caused the golem to pause, as if unsure of what to do. It stood motionless and half-rotated to surmise the wreckage.

They all listened as the demon child's cries died off slowly, only to be replaced by a low roar. The noise rose to an inhuman howl as a giant wolf tore free of the cruiser's remnants.

The golem saw this beast as the new threat. The monster raised its arms and the silver hoses lashed outwards, but the wolf pounced with little concern for its own safety.

Beast struck machine and the two inhuman adversaries battled one another. They fought with claws finding gray flesh and silver needles slicing into muscle and bone. This embrace took the pair across the field as each struggled to subdue the other.

Transfixed by the mystery of how Pyles had changed without the jar, neither Fogie moved.

"It's him all right, but how? How has he done this? What magic did he work?" Wadim said.

Together, they hobbled toward what remained of the dugout. Bronagh wanted to find anything she could use as a weapon, and Wadim followed her. On the concrete by the shredded driver-side door, she noticed an aluminum bat that must have been tucked away under the benches. Glass crunched under her foot and Bronagh came upon the broken remains of the jar. Next to it, a puddle of brownish placenta-looking ooze congealed around a tiny wing. The wing looked as though it had been chewed upon like a chicken bone.

Upon seeing this, Bronagh didn't need any vision or spirit to tell her what Pyles had done. Blinded by hate or fear, injured and maybe barely alive, he had caught the escaping hell spawn. Somehow Pyles, not knowing else to do, had caught and devoured the creature from the jar. Pyles had consumed the squirming humanoid and apparently absorbed enough of the raw ether to permanently induce a change.

Wadim staggered to the cruiser and grinned in the glow of the fire as he raised the gas can. "Next time they go down, I'm going to douse that thing and use this to light it…"

He took the bat and wrapped it in garden hose before igniting the end like a torch. His uneven shifting showed him to still be disoriented. Bronagh watched and held her breath.

The wolf and the golem battered each other toward third base. Clearly, even in its damaged state, the machine held the advantage. It didn't have to labor for breath, and its muscles didn't know fatigue or stress. Minute by bloody minute, it drew closer to ending the fight.

Pyles, the wolf, finally made a mistake, and the silver needles ruptured his sides and pierced several vital organs as they exited his chest. Like a pair of elevator cables, they moved him up and down, driving him into the ground. The golem's hoses battered Pyles against the hard earth before raising him triumphantly overhead.

Bronagh clung to Wadim and said, "It's killing him. We have to do something."

"Hit it with the gas," Wadim yelled. "While it's busy, there won't be another chance."

"But what about Pyles?" Bronagh moaned, already guessing at the answer.

"This is what he would want," Wadim replied. "We don't have time to argue."

A sobbing Bronagh moved across the baseball field and splashed the golem's chest with gasoline from the can. Before she could dump the rest, the hoses slammed Pyles down, just missing her. Bronagh stumbled back and met Pyles's pained stare with one of her own.

Bronagh saw beyond the yellow eyes of the wolf to the man behind the monster. They exchanged a second of unspoken remorse for all the hard words and tough decisions. Pyles reached as if for Bronagh, but instead jammed one clawed finger through the gas can. The hoses lifted him once more, and Pyles brought the perforated gas can along. The damaged can rained the last of its contents over the golem.

Wadim moved in with the flaming bat, but Bronagh grabbed his wrist, almost causing him to drop it. "We can't do anything till Pyles gets clear," she said.

Wadim twisted his arm to shake her grip loose. "We can't take the risk. Pyles knows we have to end this. Don't make his sacrifice worthless."

"But we can't," Bronagh said.

Wadim took a firm hold of the bat and stepped past her. He put the tip of the flaming hose into a splash of gas spotting the field and the flames erupted all around them.

Wadim chucked the flaming bat at the golem's feet and watched as it ignited the fuel. The results were a swirl of fire, followed by the *pop* of the parched grass going up under the golem's ancient boots.

The golem showed an unexpected cunning and tried to raise itself out of the blaze by using Pyles and the hoses as a counterweight. With the last of his strength, Pyles summoned every ounce of bestial fury. With the final surge of supernatural power, he grabbed one of the silver needles connecting him to the golem and pulled them both into the heart of the fire.

The combination of fir, old dusty clothes, and gas turned the budding blaze into an inferno. The golem made one last attempt to crawl free, but Pyles held it there, even as the flames consumed them.

"Pyles, no!" Bronagh screamed.

She lunged forward, but Wadim took her in his arms. He forced her face into his chest and kept her there. He held her steady and slowly walked them away from the growing pyre.

"Don't look," Wadim said. "Pyles wouldn't want you to watch this."

Wadim's words carried truth, and he saved Bronagh from many nightmares. There was a burden of making sure it was finished. He owed it to Conole and Pyles to ensure their deaths weren't in vain.

Wadim forced himself to watch until the fire had turned friend and foe alike into blacken husks. Bronagh sobbed into his shirt, and Wadim waited for whatever would come next. Death, he believed, was always the answer to the question eventually, just death.

Chapter 21

The boy's birthday party turned out to be a balloon extravaganza. Dozens of them, in all shapes and sizes, and some of which read "Get Better Nana." The festivities also included party favors of a children's character Bronagh had never heard of. Though the celebration ended up a few weeks overdue, the boy never complained. Not when his favorite nana had been released from the hospital and could now play with him.

In the aftermath, the families, the authorities, and everyone had questions, but as she was an elderly person, Bronagh explained she couldn't rightly remember. "Rightly" had been an expression of Pyles's and Bronagh found it especially to her liking. Employing it regularly did the trick of ending the countless inquiries, of which there were surprisingly few.

Wadim had been there to help field some of the serious quandaries, but thanks to the aid of the neighboring Deer Rose Police Department, a lot of the probing was tucked away into the vault of small-town secrets. Apparently, the jar had the secondary power of memory loss, and those in the station the night of their arrest couldn't recall what had happened. The whole ordeal ended up being heaped upon what were considered a few crooked police officers. Bronagh thought there was something fitting about this.

As the insurance claims adjustor from the apartment complex might have said it best when he finished his interview: "Life will go on, and that's what's important."

This Bronagh couldn't agree with more, and there was still so much to look forward to in the coming years. She realized this now that she had come to terms with the fact death didn't have to be scary. It also most certainly wasn't the end, regardless of how it came about.

Old, infirm, or wandering lost, everything here served as short stops on the long road going into the next life, the place where loved ones and friends waited. Bronagh had come to believe this will all her heart.

She had come close to losing her life, but she was on the mend and getting better every day. Her body had taken a beating at the police station and at the ballpark. There was also the matter of her stomach cancer the doctors miraculously diagnosed as gone after several days of tests and observation. Bronagh could have shared her secret cure, but she doubted anyone there would believe her.

A bandaged Bronagh held her youngest grandson while he blew out his candles and made his wish. A text message on her new phone caused her to take a short break outside before the presents were opened. She didn't have to go any further than the end of the block to see Wadim's car parked on the corner of the street.

Wadim put a hand out of the driver's window and emphatically waved. He leaned over and shouted, "I've got something you have to see, old gal."

Bronagh joined Wadim inside the car, glad to see him showing enthusiasm for something other than cheap wine. Pyles and Conole had been quietly cremated and together, Wadim and Bronagh had spread their ashes along the forest. They thought each would have appreciated this.

Afterward Wadim enjoyed wine more and more. It had become a concern he maybe wanted to drink himself to death.

The lingering effects of touching the jar had lessened over time, but Wadim still looked like a few years had been taken off him. Bronagh's pain hadn't returned, and her doctor used the phrase "remission" as priest might say the word "miracle." She didn't know if the cancer was gone for good, but life was too short to worry forever.

"How is the party going?" he asked.

Bronagh smiled and touched a strand of hair that had pushed free from her bun. "It's exactly what I needed, but your text said you said you wanted to talk. Is everything all right?"

Wadim removed a piece of paper from the glove compartment and gave it to her. He let Bronagh have a moment to read the computer printout of an online auction. Her eyes widened as she arrived at one of the objects up for sale.

"A supposed winged crypto preserved inside a glass jar, a relic from war-torn Germany, and a secret weapon of the Third

Reich. The devilish-looking cadaver has provoked legends of curses and of the darkest magic. This amazing item can be yours by clicking the urgent purchase button. Wadim, tell me you didn't. How is this even possible? The jar and the fetus inside were destroyed."

A surprisingly sober Wadim said, "I know you shut the Fogies' website down, but I reopened it. I've been doing some searching and found this. There are pictures, and they look identical to the thing Pyles consumed."

A confused Bronagh could only shake her head. "How?"

"I'm not sure, but I theorize either there is perhaps more than one. A frightening idea, I know. Or even more frightening, disposing of this thing somehow cast it back across the sea to wherever the Cloves found it in the first place. Like some grand reset button, as if its passing is treated like a tripped breaker, only to be flipped back on again across the ocean."

Bronagh crumpled the paper and couldn't hide the trembling in her arms. "So then it was all for nothing?"

"Maybe not nothing," Wadim whispered. "We could buy it, and make sure it's never used for dark purposes again. We could do it differently this time, be different in our agenda."

"No," Bronagh said, biting her lip to stop the tears. "If this thing's life is a cycle of continual resets, then maybe this is a part of it. It could be its game, and it's still trying to manipulate us to some dark end. I say no, leave it across the seas and hope wherever it is, its influence is reduced."

Wadim uncurled the painful fist Bronagh had made. "Are you sure? Your sickness could always return."

Bronagh took Wadim's hand and pressed it into her belly. "Yes, I am sure. The sickness may come back, or it may not. Either way, life is short. This may be a blessing I never considered. Good friends and family have come and gone, and I wouldn't want an eternity to grieve them or to lose my ability to care. Yes, immortality would be fine, but can you really call it living if that's what it brings? No, Wadim, I'm fine enjoying the time left to us. That's what you should do instead of crawling inside a bottle."

The last part stung him enough that Wadim flinched. "I long for the eternal nights of not caring for those that come and go. I guess though you make a point about not wanting to spend forever that way. I wish the end didn't have to always be so final."

"It wouldn't be the end if it wasn't," Bronagh said.

They sat in silence for a moment and watched some last-minute party guests arrive up the street. A gaggle of the celebrating children had made it to the lawn, where they chased one another with squirt guns. Bronagh and Wadim watched for a while, enjoying the moment and each other's company.

"Well, that's enough spectating. We should go join them. It looks fun," Bronagh said.

Wadim tried to protest, but Bronagh tugged on his arm until he relented. They made it in time to be in the birthday

boy's big picture, and neither of the Fogies had ever smiled
wider in their lives.

The end.

Coming Soon...

The Shadows They Cast

A collection of horror short stories.

www.ingramcontent.com/pod-product-compliance
Lightning Source LLC
Chambersburg PA
CBHW051954150726
47999CB00004B/1376